To Catch a Prince

To Catch a Prince

Gillian McKnight

Simon & Schuster Books for Young Readers
New York ~ London ~ Toronto ~ Sydney

SIMON & SCHUSTER BOOKS FOR YOUNG READERS

An imprint of Simon & Schuster Children's Publishing Division

1230 Avenue of the Americas, New York, New York 10020

SIMON & SCHUSTER BOOKS FOR YOUNG READERS is a trademark of Simon & Schuster, Inc.

Book design by Jessica Sonkin

The text for this book is set in Adobe Garamond.

Manufactured in the United States of America

2 4 6 8 10 9 7 5 3 1

CIP data for this book is available from the Library of Congress.

ISBN 0-689-87733-1

To Corinna Cappetti-Klein

1

♔

Plan B

THE MAN SEATED in the middle of row twenty-three had bad breath. But that wasn't the problem. He also had agoraphobia, which made it absolutely impossible for him to sit on the aisle, with all the rushing carts and babies. And he had vertigo, which made it out of the question for him to sit by the window and look out at the billowing clouds. So the man in the middle separated Helene Masterson from Alexis Worth on their first-ever transatlantic flight.

That was the problem.

If Alexis leaned forward to talk to Helene, Mr. Middle flinched. And if Helene passed a note to Alexis, he grumbled about his "personal, paid-for space." Helene politely asked him to switch seats with her, but he refused, slipped on a black eye mask, and stuck an earplug in each ear to cement the point. He reclined in his seat and breathed his bad breath.

Now, this would be tolerable on some flights—from LA to San Francisco, say, or Washington to Boston. But New York to London was almost seven hours, and sixteen-year-olds Helene and Alexis had a busy schedule planned for their time in the air. They would play cards at first. Then they'd eat their preordered specialty meals (vegetarian for Helene, diet for Alexis). And then, dinner finished, they would switch to a careful study of all their favorite magazines. They'd even arrived at JFK two and a half hours early to have time to buy one of every magazine on the shelf. They *had* to be able to sit together.

"What if I put the window shade down?" Helene said to Mr. Middle. She wasn't sure if he could hear her with his earplugs in, so in a louder voice she added, "Then could you sit by the window? You have those things on your eyes anyway."

"I *told* you, young lady," Mr. Middle replied, the earplugs making him speak in an extra loud, extra annoying voice, "I have *paid* for a middle seat, and I will *sit* in the middle seat."

Alexis tried not to make a face, but then she realized Mr. Middle couldn't see her, so she stuck out her tongue and rolled her eyes up into her head. Helene laughed, and then turned her giggles into a cough. She didn't want to annoy Mr. Middle any further.

Reaching into her backpack, Helene pulled out her sketch pad and some pens. She spelled a message out to Alexis, under-lining it twice. PLAN B!

Alexis nodded and smiled slightly. From her Coach purse she took out lip gloss and blush. Plan B always required a little sprucing up. Then she winked at Helene, stored her tray table, and stood up from her seat.

They'd created Plan B a few years earlier when they were still in junior high. Back then, if Helene and Alexis were fighting, as best friends will occasionally do, their parents would separate them. Helene would be sent to one room and Alexis to another, and neither would get the last Häagen-Dazs bar. It was, as Helene said, "a lose-lose situation." So they decided that whenever they fought, they would make up before the grown-ups stepped in. One of them just had to whisper "Plan B," and they'd stop. That way they both were allowed to vacation on Martha's Vineyard, skate at Rockefeller Center, hold a swimming party in the backyard, eat half the ice cream bar.

Plan B worked in other situations too. If Alexis was unsuccessfully trying to get an extension for a history paper, she'd text Helene an urgent <u>PLAN B</u>! Helene would immediately go to the classroom and reason with the teacher until it was clear that Alexis was actually doing the teacher a favor by not turning in her homework on time. See, what Helene knew—and nobody else did—was that Alexis grew uncomfortably shy around adults, especially mother types. She would just turn speechless sometimes. Not because she was stupid or scared, just intimidated in a way that nobody but Helene understood. But Helene's charm plus Alexis's beauty worked like magic.

Now Helene watched from her window seat as Alexis, in the aisle, flicked her glossy hair and stared at the flight attendant with the twin lakes of her blue eyes. But the flight attendant, busy dishing out Diet Cokes and those miniature glass bottles off a clanking trolley, ignored her. After a moment Alexis shrugged and gesticulated sort of spastically in an expression of defeat. This meant it was Helene's turn.

"Excuse me," Helene told Mr. Middle, tapping him gently on the shoulder. He flinched. "I just need to squeeze by."

Mr. Middle didn't move. The flight attendant had both hands on her cart handle and was looking at Alexis impatiently. Desperate, Helene hurdled Mr. Middle's legs and tumbled into the aisle.

"I'm so sorry," she said, collecting herself as best she could. Then she whispered into the flight attendant's ear, "I think our exuberance about our first transatlantic flight is bothering this poor man. Is there any way we could get two seats together?"

The pinched-lip flight attendant cracked a smile as she took in the scene: an extremely white-knuckled Mr. Middle and a very dimpled, very straight-toothed, smiling Alexis. At this point in the plan, Alexis's role was simply to smile. She was the picture of innocence.

"Well, it just so happens I *do* have two seats together," the flight attendant said, trying unsuccessfully to hold on to her usual frown. She leaned in close to the girls and whispered conspiratorially, "But they're in first class. I'm sure you don't mind."

"Oh, no, we don't mind at all," Helene said.

Alexis's smile grew even wider.

Good-bye, Mr. Middle.

If you spotted Helene and Alexis in a store, you'd never guess they were best friends. Alexis would be headed for the dressing room with six items that perfectly accentuated her current wardrobe. She'd be the tall, beautiful girl that everyone—girls and boys—stared at. Her long, straight dark hair would be up in a smooth ponytail, and something about her distant, distracted concentration would make you think you recognized her—was she the model in the J.Crew catalog? in a Kodak commercial? Helene, on the other hand, would have found the one totally impractical item in the store—maybe high-heeled leopard-skin rain boots or a lavender tutu—and she'd take it to the checkout counter without trying it on. Then, while waiting for Alexis to choose her clothes carefully, Helene would wrap the salesman around her little finger. While ringing up her purchase, he would suddenly announce that that particular tutu, or those and only those rain boots, just happened to be on sale. He would then give her what Alexis referred to as the "Helene discount."

It might be twenty percent off, or an invitation to a party to see the new spring collections before anyone else. Or as illustrated in this particular case, an upgrade to first class.

Helene wasn't gorgeous like Alexis, but she sparkled. Her hair ran in messy curls down her back. She was as punk-rock as Alexis was preppy. While Alexis wore cashmere sweaters and Juicy jeans with pointed boots, Helene wore combat boots with vintage dresses. While Alexis had added the most perfect tritonal highlights to her black-as-night hair, Helene managed to turn the tub, the dog, and a swatch of her tawny hair a bright, bubblegum pink. Alexis's friends wore matching sweater sets and played tennis. Helene was friends with everyone else—the sleepy stoners and the geeky math whizzes and the jocks who threw the most out-of-control parties.

So what did they have in common? A mom (Helene's). A dad (Alexis's). A dog, a house, the backseat of a Lexus (Dad's), and an Audi (Mom's), not to mention the Nissan Pathfinder they'd received when they got their learner's permits.

See, Helene and Alexis were more than best friends. They were stepsisters. Eight years earlier, when the girls were only eight, Helene and her mom, Brenda Masterson, moved from sunny California to live with Alexis and her father, Hugo Worth, in Scarsdale, a wealthy, leafy suburb of New York City. At first the girls were wary of each other. Alexis wouldn't let Helene touch her Madame Alexander dolls, and Helene spent the days riding her skateboard around and around the huge circular driveway.

But then Hugo, who spent his workday sculpting the public images of corporations and celebrities, brought both girls to his office—just when Madonna happened to be there.

Okay, let's try that again: Hugo Worth, PR star and undoubtedly the coolest dad ever, ushered his two lovely daughters into his superswank Tribeca office to meet the Princess of Pop—no, no, the Queen of the Universe as she is known by anyone with a brain—the woman whose name naturally belongs in boldface type, Madonna herself.

Over pizza and ice cream afterward, the girls found themselves talking nonstop about their newly autographed photos, their favorite celebrities, and their mutual fear of three-hundred-pound men with beards and sunglasses. (Madonna had been flanked by four such fellows.) They found that they understood each other like no one else did. Helene could talk to Alexis about missing her father, who spent every day sitting on a beach in Malibu, writing a screenplay and wearing a Speedo. He always called Helene a day late for her birthday, had to be reminded twice to pick her up at the airport during her winter visits, and always forgot the Christmas tree. Alexis could tell Helene about her own absentee parent, a mother who hadn't even requested custody during the trial. She'd asked only for the BMW.

Imagine: stepsisters who loved each other, best friends who lived together. At school they had distinct groups of friends, but at the end of the day they sat on the living room floor and discussed everything. During those hours their parents called them by one name: Helenalexis. There was no separating them.

The fact of the matter was, Mr. Middle never stood a chance.

2

Everything's Better in First Class

IF THEY HADN'T moved to first class, they wouldn't have met Tony, and if they hadn't met Tony, they wouldn't have seen the picture, and if they hadn't seen the picture, well, then the entire summer would have been different. Ruined? Maybe. Or maybe saved. But in any case, Plan B got them there, as it always did. But as usually happened, they didn't have a plan to get themselves out of whatever trouble Plan B happened to bring.

Helene had spent her early years living in a school bus on Venice Beach while her father "got his feet wet" in the Hollywood scene, so she claimed not to care about luxury. But even she had to admit it: Everything was better in first class. The seats were leather and wide enough for her to kick her shoes off and curl up. At lunchtime they were served arugula salad with salmon on real china, with real flatware. They were asked, "Would you like sparkling water with your meal?" And they had a male flight attendant placing a real rose on their tray tables. And he was cute.

"More than cute," Alexis said. "He's *hot*."

In her journal, Alexis the perfectionist had made a list of the attributes she wanted in a guy. He should be taller than she was (Alexis was five foot seven). He should have dark hair just like hers, so their children would have dark hair and the entire family would match on Christmas cards. He should have nice, thoughtful eyes, preferably green. He should be athletic, but not dumb. He should have impeccable manners. He should be sweet.

Tony, the hot flight attendant, folded a napkin over one arm as he poured their San Pellegrino, so of course he had manners. And when he cleared their dishes, a lock of black hair tumbled over his forehead, almost hiding his eyes, which happened to be the color of Helene's jade locket. Deep, delicious green. His shoulders were broad, and he was so tall he could place Alexis's carry-on in the overhead bin without reaching or straining, even though the Prada satchel was stacked high with *Elle, People, Vogue,* and *W.*

Best of all, he spoke with an English accent.

"Ladies," he asked, "care for a touch more sparkling water?"

"Yes, sir," Alexis giggled.

"Please," he replied, reaching to refill her glass, "call me Tony."

"Well, Tony, I'm Alexis, and this is my sister, Helene, and we're going to London."

"I would hope so," Tony said, winking, "because this plane is headed there, and I have a cabin full of passengers who'd be very upset if we had to turn around. Now tell me. Are you going there to shop? Because I know the most *secret* place where they sell Prada overstock."

"Actually," Helene replied, "we're going for the whole summer. I have an internship with the National Gallery." She tried to keep the pride out of her voice. Helene had known for years that she wanted to be an artist, probably a painter (although lately sculpting was looking pretty cool too), and she'd been chosen out of hundreds of applicants to fly to London and work at the country's most prestigious art museum for three months. Alexis had come along, of course, because they couldn't imagine a summer separated. But she didn't have any plans. Except to shop, of course, and maybe catch a horse show at Gatcombe Park. Still, she wasn't going to tell Tony that.

"And I"—Alexis's pause sounded dramatic, but she was really just trying to think of something to say—"have an internship at *Vogue.*" This was a total lie. The closest Alexis had come to *Vogue* was the copy she held in her hands. But it was hard for her sometimes, when Helene succeeded at every academic thing she tried. People thought nothing bothered Alexis because she looked so perfect and calm and because she succeeded in so many things—beauty, sports, style. But no one, not even Helene, understood how much she worried if things were out of place—if she didn't eat her particular diet meal, if her clothes were out of fashion, if she couldn't find the right makeup, if she lost a horse show. She felt as if her whole life would fall apart before her eyes if she lost any ounce of control. Sometimes she wondered what it would be like to be Helene, who never had anything in place, was always a total mess, but still always seemed happy. Sometimes, and she was quite ashamed of this, Alexis even envied her.

"Such talented girls," Tony said, clearly impressed. "Can I offer you anything else to make your flight as delightful as possible?"

"What I'd love," Helene said, "is whatever he's having." She pointed to a rather delightful looking pink beverage in a tall, frosted glass.

"Well, darlings, I'm afraid you'll have to wait a couple of years for that, but we could swing something even better. It just so happens that J. Lo was on this flight last, and we had to special-order ingredients for milk shakes. You know how she is. I'll whip you each up one." Tony winked and walked up the aisle. Alexis sighed. "Tony is such a nice name, don't you think? Although I'd probably call him Anthony. How old do you think he is?"

Helene giggled. Clearly Alexis had a crush on Tony—she never would have made up that ridiculous lie about *Vogue* if she didn't. *Poor Tony,* Helene thought. When Alexis got a crush, it usually ended badly—for the boy. Guys couldn't resist Alexis when she turned her attention on them. Her crushes might last just a few days, but the boys were smitten for years. But as Helene watched Tony adjusting the window shade a few rows up, she suddenly realized he would probably survive Alexis's affections.

"Alexis, listen," she said, "I don't want to destroy your fantasy or anything, but think about it. Tony's a flight attendant. He knows designer labels. He's totally buff, gorgeous, and exquisitely well groomed. He's . . ."

As Helene attempted to explain these rather obvious signs, Alexis's eyes followed Tony as he walked toward them. She pinched Helene's thigh lightly to get her attention.

"Don't pinch me!" Helene said loudly. "It's not my fault you didn't notice he's gay. He's so *clearly* gay."

Alexis cleared her throat loudly and raised her eyebrows, indicating something—or someone—just above Helene's head. Helene looked up, slowly. She had a pretty good idea of what she would see. There was Tony, one row ahead. He held two gigantic chocolate milk shakes with extra whipped cream, and he stared directly at her. She felt mortified. She had to act quickly.

"God, not that I care," she said. "I mean, my best friend is gay. Alexis, you know that. David's gay, and he's totally my best friend."

Tony lowered his head and raised his arched eyebrows at her, giving what she deemed a highly disapproving look. Helene's stomach churned. *Okay, that was probably the dumbest recovery ever. You sound like a total homophobe.* But it was true! She did have a best friend who was really a gay guy. *Well, here we go,* she thought.

"So, Helene," he demanded in a stern voice, "your 'best friend' is gay?"

Helene nodded lamely.

Tony's stern demeanor cracked, and a smile flashed across his face. "Is he single?"

After that they had an ally. Tony brought them extra down pillows. He brought Helene a second milk shake; Alexis, who was on a never-ending diet, longingly eyed both the milk shake and Tony. Later she would refer to it as the most important thirty-minute relationship of her life. But right now, being a pragmatic girl, she decided to quell her sorrows with a second milk shake. Who could think about calories when the totally hot, stud flight attendant couldn't fall victim to her charms?

When Alexis had finished all of *Elle* and *Vogue* and *W,* and Helene had grown just the teensiest bit bored of *Wuthering Heights* (she knew Cathy was supposed to be a romantic heroine and all, but God, she was kind of a witch, too), Tony brought out the best treat. A cake-sized stack of British tabloids. "Really, girls," he said, "if you plan to be in London, you must know London gossip. Enough of this Justin Timberlake. Who cares about Ashton Coochie, or whatever his name is? Let's consider some real celebrities!"

It was while Alexis was reading about British fashion (which according to Tony had its heyday during the punk-rock seventies) that Helene spotted *him*. The man who had secretly captured her imagination for the past two years: Prince William. He was outside, on a rugby pitch. The prince must have just stopped running, because his dirty-blond hair was sprouting up in all directions and his cheeks were flushed. His jaw was like the prow of a boat. But it was his eyes that did it. The blue of the Mediterranean. These eyes didn't tease like her recent boyfriend Jeremy's did, always darting the other way, never making contact. William's eyes caught hers. She knew, Helene *knew,* that he was actually looking at a camera lens, like he'd been doing his whole life. She *knew* that he was just a guy, and so he was probably thinking about a hamburger and a beer. She knew this was a piece of paper. She *knew* she was suffering from a serious brain freeze. But still he spoke to her.

You've got things going on beneath your surface, Helene. You're like the moors, wild and deep.

Helene smiled. "Hey," she whispered at the magazine, "I am?"

Alexis, thinking Helene had said something to her, asked, "Huh? What?"

"Oh, nothing," Helene said. She smiled, embarrassed. What in the world was wrong with her?

The girls' decision to fly to London had been rushed (which was the only reason Hugo Worth hadn't found them first-class seats to begin with). Helene had heard from the National Gallery in late April. She and Alexis had arranged to take exams early, meaning Helene would have to pass up the last-minute trip to Los Angeles to visit her father. And Alexis would have to pass up the yacht tour of the Bahamas with her mother. These might sound like sweet vacations, but it's pretty hard to have a good time when you're alone with a parent who forgets what grade you're in. And even worse, since they were cramming for exams the entire month of May, the girls hadn't spent any time together—and they were strangely out of touch.

For example, Alexis still didn't know why dreadlocked Jeremy had broken up with Helene the same night he declared his undying love for her in a poetry slam at the local coffee shop; a teary Helene had simply refused to talk about it. Nor did she know that the reason Helene's tears disappeared as suddenly as they'd come was that her punky, gregarious, ever-popular sister had set her sights on none other than Prince William.

For her part, Helene was honestly embarrassed about her crush. After all, he was a prince (duh), and she was just a high school girl who looked nothing like the wispy waifs the prince was seen with in the magazines she so religiously read. But she couldn't help it. After Jeremy, she longed for a sophisticated guy. Someone who understood her and her feelings. Her father lived far away in California, and she knew it was a bit of a relief for him when she moved to the East Coast. She knew that her family life would seem like a cakewalk next to Prince William's, but maybe he would stop pawing at her for two seconds to listen. Jeremy seemed to have just one thing on his mind at all times. She wanted someone who was more exotic than Scarsdale, not to mention more authentic than Jeremy's dreadlocks. Plus William was gorgeous. He was stellar—her new favorite word.

Helene had done all her research between exam cram sessions and by the time exams were over, Helene had a clear set of goals for the summer. She would lose five pounds by eating fewer carbs. (Good-bye, lovely muffins and bagels!) She would visit all the museums, going twice to the Victoria and Albert because it was so huge. She would run along the Thames to find inspiration for her new series of watercolors, which she called *Motion*. She would sit in cafés and sketch everyone who came in. But most of all, she would meet him, William. And seeing him in this magazine while on her way to England must be a sign, she thought. There would be a connection between them instantly; she just knew it. Given the right opportunity, she could do it. She could catch a prince.

"I have something to tell you, Lexy. I have a crush on a guy in London."

"*No way!* You're so smart! Tell me all about him." Alexis assumed that Helene had met a guy in a chatroom; Helene was smart enough to snag the one cool guy on the Internet and weed out all the creeps. If Alexis had thought of finding a boy ahead of time, she'd have something specific to look forward to. It's not that she wasn't excited about London. But think about it: She'd be spending the days with her dad's credit card, while Helene met talented, fascinating—not to mention hot—artists (in Alexis's imagination, all painters were male, gorgeous, and wore only spattered Carhartt's). It was a little depressing.

"Well, I've only seen his picture. He's tall. And he has these amazing blue eyes. He's outdoorsy. He likes to be in nature and all. Definitely not like Jeremy."

Realizing she was describing William exactly as he was pictured in the magazine, Helene closed it swiftly.

But Alexis noticed. "Hey, let me see that."

She flipped open to the picture Helene had been gazing at. She looked at William. Then back at Helene. Then at William again.

"Helene . . . no!"

Helene nodded sheepishly.

"Prince William? The-son-of-Diana-and-Charles Prince William? The-heir-to-the-throne-of-England Prince William?"

"Well, technically Charles is the heir apparent—"

"*People* magazine's sexiest-man-alive Prince William? *That* Prince William?"

"Uh, yeah."

Alexis's pointed questions were starting to intrude on Helene's fantasy, and she half wished she'd never said anything. Luckily, Tony arrived just then with a fresh round of milk shakes. She picked up hers and sipped at it in stony silence for a moment. But this was Alexis, and before their drinks were halfway gone, Helene had confessed everything. How it had started as a stupid fantasy. But how as she'd learned more about him, she'd realized they were perfect for each other. Really, if he weren't so far away, she thought they'd have hit it off already. But now Helene was on her way to London, and she'd recently received a piece of amazing news: In late June, the National Gallery would hold its inaugural Royal Ball. Prince Charles was a dedicated patron of the arts, so there was no doubt in Helene's mind that he would attend. And knowing what she knew about Prince William, he surely wouldn't pass up the chance to go to a ball filled with beautifully dressed ladies!

"So William will be there," Helene finished breathlessly, "and I'll be there. And I'll wear some gorgeous dress—please please *please* tell me you'll help me pick it out—and he'll be in a tux, of course, or a morning suit. You know, with a plaid cummerbund or something, and tails, and those funny little shoes."

"Spats," Alexis said, correcting her sister. She sipped at her glass, but it was empty. "They're called spats, and they're not technically shoes but gaiters that cover the shoes."

"Well, *whatever* they are," Helene said, "he'll be wearing them, and well, I made a promise to myself. I'm going to get a kiss from Prince William that will make me forget Jeremy ever existed."

Maybe it was all that sugar. Maybe it was that Helene had never bothered to confide to Alexis why she and Jeremy broke up. Or maybe it was that Helene had an internship and a crush and a plan for the summer, and Alexis had nothing but a stack of silly magazines on her lap and Hugo's credit card in her wallet. Whatever it was, Alexis soon found herself telling Helene that she could never score a hottie like Prince William. She knew she should be asking sensitive questions about Jeremy and the breakup, but instead she felt like screaming. Why should Helene get everything? The grades? The job? The guy? And not just any guy, but *Prince William?* It was just too much.

"Listen, One-Three-One," Alexis heard herself saying, using the name she called Helene only when she was really annoyed with her (it referred to the number that had appeared on the scale beneath Helene's feet, followed immediately by a scream of despair). "I don't know how to tell you this, but you're just not his type. I happen to know that royalty in general, and the prince in particular, doesn't like bookish, nerdy girls."

Helene stared at Alexis in disbelief. She'd seen this jealous, haughty side of Alexis only occasionally. Often it covered up Alexis's true shyness and came out only at school, especially around guys. But it had never been turned on Helene quite like this before.

Alexis wasn't finished. "And I've been meaning to tell you, One-Three-One, you're getting sort of *zaftig* again. Not exactly the right look for the girlfriend of the future king of England." To emphasize her point, Alexis stuck a hand over the armrest and pinched Helene's stomach.

Helene giggled, though she was also a little annoyed.

"Oh, and I suppose you think someone like you would be perfect for him," Helene snapped back. "Perfect body, perfect hair, no zits ever. Well, *Pinocchio,* William would never have you. You're . . . you're . . . you're . . ." She hesitated, trying to find fault with her flawless sister. Finally she belted out, "You're surgically altered. What do you think the prince would say if he saw some before-and-after pictures of a certain *nose job?*"

Alexis cringed. They never mentioned the nose job in public, and Alexis had told friends at school that she'd broken it while riding a horse.

"At least I'm not some grungy wannabe punk rocker."

"Yeah? Well, Leo still liked *me* better," Helene shot back, grabbing the magazine out of her sister's hands.

"That's only because *I* wasn't there," Alexis said.

It was true. The Saturday Leonardo DiCaprio had stopped over to have an emergency image consult with Hugo Worth, Alexis just happened to have an equestrian show, and Helene alone got to sit poolside with the star, sipping iced tea in her new tankini. Before he left he signed a picture for her: *To heavenly Helene, a true friend. You're admirer, Leo.* Alexis wouldn't leave her room for a whole day when she found out. Helene had the photo framed.

"I'm just saying," Helene repeated, "Leo liked me a lot."

"Don't even mention his name," Alexis said, holding up her hand. "Besides, he's just an *actor.* He doesn't even know the difference between 'your' and 'you are'—he doesn't exactly have the refinement of a prince."

Helene found herself thinking of Plan B—Plan B and a good nap to soothe the sugar-induced headache that was pounding her temples. But instead of calling a truce, she heard herself saying, "Care to make it interesting, Pinocchio?"

Alexis, who looked about as bleary as Helene felt, still managed to pout her perfect lips and blow an enchantingly errant lock of hair off her face. Then she said, "Explain yourself, One-Three-One."

Helene spat the words out quickly, before she could think better of them: "One of us has to catch Prince William by the end of the summer."

Alexis found herself wishing for the security of Plan B just as much as Helene was. But instead she stared into Helene's hazel eyes and said, "Three months to catch a prince? Where's your sense of pride, One-Three-One? I bet you I can kiss him inside six weeks."

Now Helene sat up straighter. Leo or no Leo, everyone thought that Alexis was simply gorgeous. But Helene was determined not to give this one to Alexis so easily. She had just as good a chance as Alexis.

"Okay, Alexis, let's be serious. We have to find and capture Prince William's heart by the end of the summer. And this means true love, not fluttering of eyelashes and pursing of lips."

Alexis frowned and looked deeply into Helene's eyes. She knew something had gone terribly wrong between Helene and Jeremy, and she wanted more than anything to know what it was. But Helene had her wall up, and Alexis knew better than to think she could get anything out of Helene now. Helene would tell her only when she was ready.

Helene gulped. She knew Alexis expected something from her. An explanation of things. But Helene just couldn't face it. She had let herself forget for a little while that Alexis didn't know what happened between Jeremy and her. For years they'd discussed even the smallest details of the boys they were interested in, from first dates, to first kisses, to the great unknown: losing their virginity. Both Alexis and Helene agreed they wouldn't do that until they were married. It was a pact they had struck back in eighth grade, when Angela Harmon's older sister Kelly had gotten pregnant. She'd never thought things would be so difficult though. That decisions could be so complicated.

"True love," Helene said. She watched as Alexis's eyes fell to her lap, and Helene felt her friend's disappointment at her choice not to confide. But then it was gone.

"So it's a bet," Alexis said, taking a deep breath and smiling.

Helene's heart was tight with anticipation and dread. She and Alexis had never been like this before. Plan B, Helenalexis, the MasterWorth Sisters—their teamwork had always fixed things. Even Hugo and Brenda had commented on how strange it was that the girls didn't compete. In fact, Brenda once wanted to send them to a therapist for their complete lack of sibling rivalry, but luckily Hugo said he could think of better ways to spend three hundred dollars an hour.

What her mother and stepfather didn't know was that Helene hated competition, so she'd grown adept at wanting things that Alexis would never want. Alexis liked to ride horses, so Helene spent her school hours volunteering at the animal shelter. Alexis had been playing tennis on the backyard clay courts since she could walk. So Helene hiked, sailed, and rode her mountain bike through the streets, and recently on a trip to the Shawangunks, Jeremy had taught her to rock climb (which she discovered is as close to flying as a person can get). Alexis signed up for AP math and chemistry (which she would kill to get a four on), while Helene took AP English and history (if she got lower than a five, she'd die).

They had their own spheres, their own niches, like the two species of ocean birds she'd learned about in biology: One fed on fish in the surf, the other on bugs in the sand.

Still, Helene had always wondered: What if one day she wanted exactly the same thing as her stepsister? What if she wanted what Alexis wanted? What would they do then? But in her wildest dreams she'd never thought that thing would be a boy, because boys—well, every boy wanted Alexis. In her heart of hearts she believed that if Alexis had been there the day Leo came over, she would have gotten the autographed picture, not Helene.

"And the loser," Alexis said, interrupting Helene's thoughts, "the loser, One-Three-One, will call the winner Your Highness for the rest of her life." She settled back in her chair. "I'm looking forward to it."

Helene gritted her teeth.

"I dunno, Alexis. 'Princess Pinocchio' doesn't exactly have a royal ring to it."

Grim-faced, the girls raised their empty, sticky glasses and were about to clink them together when Tony appeared. He had an amused expression on his face, and both girls blushed when they realized that he—and everyone else in first class—had probably heard every ridiculous thing they'd just said.

"No, no, no," Tony said. "A bet is something you shake on. Glasses are for toasting. Now put down your drinks, and shake hands like men. Or rather, like princesses-to-be."

Alexis extended her right hand. Helene giggled as she grasped it in hers, but inside she was nervous, and she could tell Alexis was too. For better or worse, the bet was on.

3

London Calling

TONY WOKE THE girls fifteen minutes before the plane landed so they would have time to freshen up. They'd fallen asleep midsentence like they usually did, and he'd tucked them into blankets, removed the magazines from their laps, and put soothing masks on their eyes to prevent circles.

"Good morning, princesses," he said as he took off their masks. But it was morning neither in London nor in Scarsdale, and Alexis was in no mood to be woken up. She sighed and grumbled as she switched her first-class cashmere socks for her own ankle socks and combed her hair. Helene, on the other hand, felt full of expectation. They were finally in London! She wanted to run off the plane and bound into the streets and take it all in. True, somewhere beneath her exuberance, she remembered something somewhat daunting had happened midflight, but she didn't want to ruin her mood. There were no signs of what had transpired earlier: The milk shake wreckage was gone, and of course, the magazine was too. But as she was leaving the plane and kissing Tony on both cheeks, Helene thought she heard him whisper, "Good luck." When she turned around to acknowledge him, he was already calling out "Good-bye" to all the departing passengers, and she was being shuffled off the plane.

Helene shook her head to clear it. She needed to focus on her main concern of this moment: recognizing her aunt Barbara and her cousin Nichola, neither of whom she had seen for eight years. Yet as soon as the girls had passed through customs and claimed their baggage, a much more glamorous version of Helene's mother came running—or what approximated running when wearing high-heeled mules and a Chanel suit—toward the girls.

Helene's mother, Brenda, appeared at times to be the exact opposite of her sister. Before she met Hugo, Helene's mother had taught classics—that is, old stuff—at Purchase College and wore the clothes of a professor or a therapist: flowing skirts and gauzy blouses, all in dark, muted colors, with sensible, back-friendly shoes and little makeup. Now she dedicated her time to improving the lives of those less fortunate, while augmenting her wardrobe with more expensive flowing skirts and gauzy blouses. But Brenda's sister, Barbara Hussein, had lived in London for the past twenty years, ever since she fell in love with Saheed, an Omani businessman, during her college semester abroad. Over time she'd picked up British mannerisms, grown used to upper-class life, dropped her Brooklyn accent for an English one, banned wrinkles with Botox, coiffed her hair like Jackie Onassis, and developed a close personal relationship with Giorgio Armani, Gianni Versace, and Marc Jacobs. But recently Barbara had started giving back to her community. Perhaps her sister had rubbed off on her a little. And, just like her sister, Barbara talked a mile a minute.

"Oh, Helene, you're all grown up. You're so beautiful," she said, kissing Helene on both cheeks. "But what on earth have you done to your hair! Pink! . . . Nichola, no ideas; don't even *think* about asking me if you can do that."

Nichola, Helene's younger cousin, seemed to approach reluctantly. Helene tried to say hello, but Barbara turned around and shouted to a short woman in a maid's uniform who carried a little boy. "Come on, Basha, hurry up and show Richard his cousin, the lovely Helene, launcher of a thousand ships. Basha's our nanny. She's fabulous. And oh, my, you must be Alexis. What a stunning girl!"

Ignoring Basha, who had approached with Richard, Barbara kissed Alexis and held her face for examination. "I last saw you at your father and Brenda's wedding. You'd stained your white flower-girl dress with grape juice, and now look at you. You could model . . . Nichola, are you noticing her posture?"

Nichola shrugged, and Barbara obliviously continued, "Dear me, Alexis, don't tell me that's all your luggage. Where will we put it? We'll have to rent another flat! I'm so sorry Saheed couldn't be here."

Suddenly she beamed and stretched out her arms. "Look! These are my delightful babies."

For the first time, Helene and Alexis examined their cousins. If Nichola was a baby, she was the grumpiest, gangliest baby ever. Helene remembered that Nichola was three years younger, making her thirteen, but she was so tall and, well, *developed,* that she looked to be the same age as the sisters. She was at least two inches taller than Barbara, and almost as tall as Alexis. And even her demure plaid pinafore and her sulky slouch couldn't hide her rather large chest. But her face was still round and childlike. She bit her thumbnail and stood with one foot crossed in front of the other. Her dark hair fell to her waist in a thick braid that was tied with a large blue ribbon.

She looked most unhappy to be at Heathrow. "Hullo," she said, barely above a whisper. "Mum said I'd like to see American girls. I was picturing something more Britney Spears."

Aunt Barbara smiled, pretending not to hear her daughter. A reaction, the girls would learn, that was her trademark.

Five-year-old Richard made up for his sister's crankiness. He wriggled out of Basha's arms and flung himself at Helene's knees. She laughed and picked him up, carrying him to the car while wearing the backpack that held all of her belongings. Alexis, Nichola, and Basha followed, struggling with Alexis's three Louis Vuitton suitcases. "Really, darling," Aunt Barbara kept saying, looking back as she led the parade, "where did you imagine we would put all of it?"

Outside the terminal a steady rain fell, and the sky, the buildings, and the cars were all shades of gray or black. Helene yelped and almost dropped her cousin. "It's stellar," she whispered to Richard, and then she screamed at Alexis, "Hurry up, it's really London. I want to see everything immediately."

"Like what? It's overcast, cold, and wet," Alexis said, catching up. She was beginning to feel intensely worried about this summer. For one thing, it didn't look or feel like summer. Maybe she should have stayed home and ridden her horses. Here she would freeze and her hair would frizz as she walked around alone, while Helene worked at her fabulous internship.

Alexis seemed so honestly miserable that Helene let her have the front seat, and she crowded into the back with Basha and the kids.

Aunt Barbara was a terrible driver. She drove very quickly, then stopped abruptly, and she never, ever stayed straight. At one point Alexis almost grabbed the wheel to keep the car in the right lane. Which over here was actually the left lane. She'd been prepared for cars driving on the opposite side of the road, but she didn't realize how awful that was for the passenger. In America, if you sat in the front passenger seat, you could check your manicure or text someone to find out when the movie was. But here, you were stuck in the driver's seat without a steering wheel. Every time the car turned right or left, it felt as if there might be a head-on collision—and there was nothing you could do about it. Not good for a control freak like Alexis. To make matters worse, Aunt Barbara had decided to take "a scenic route home."

"Look up, girls. Do you know what that is?" she kept saying.

"No way! It's really the Houses of Parliament! Can you slow down so I can see better?" Helene would shout from the backseat.

"And what is that?" asked Aunt Barbara, narrowly missing being rear-ended by a double-decker bus.

"Big Ben! I can't wait to hear it."

"And that?" Aunt Barbara asked, as she jerked the car out of the way of an oncoming taxi.

"We're driving along the Thames, just like the view Monet painted. It's all hazy and lovely."

Alexis's skin felt chapped and badly in need of moisturizer. The rain hitting the windshield made her think about being cooped up in Aunt Barbara's flat all summer while her friends back home played tennis and lounged by the pool. What was she thinking? Alexis despised rain. So far, she despised London. She was so unbearably tired; her head became too heavy to hold upright. As she closed her eyes, she heard Helene say, "Could you just drive by Trafalgar Square? That would make me sooo happy."

Just as Alexis drifted off to sleep, she thought, *At least I'm not here on my own. At least I have Helene. And*—she remembered with a jolt—*one of us will have William.*

Alexis didn't worry about competition at all. In fact, she thrived on it—tennis tournaments, horse shows, student council. Catching William would be just another contest. *May the best girl win,* she thought with a smile.

4

Puppies and Ducks and Horses, Oh My!

JET LAG WORKS in mysterious ways. Earlier that day they'd been so exhausted they could hardly sip the watery soup offered them before collapsing in the twin beds of the immaculate guest room. They'd awoken for periodic attempts at unpacking before landing back in bed. Now, at five in the morning, Helene whispered to her sister, "Alexis, are you awake?"

Usually it was dangerous to talk to Alexis before nine A.M. Unless she'd taken her shower, applied her makeup, dried her hair, and drunk her first Diet Coke, she might throw a pillow at you. But this time Alexis answered cheerily, "Totally awake— and totally starving."

"To the kitchen, to the kitchen," Helene commanded, and as they snuck out in their pajamas, closing the door quietly behind them, they laughed at how funny it was to sneak around Aunt Barbara's house. For one thing, they had no idea where they were going. Where *was* the kitchen? They had been led like sleepwalkers to their room yesterday by Basha, and nothing looked familiar. Helene turned left, down a hallway that was lined with green-striped wallpaper and jutting oil lanterns flickering mysteriously. The walls were covered with portraits of poodles, hundreds of them, all in oil paint and set in heavy gilded frames. The girls didn't dare try the four closed doors along this hallway, so they continued straight until the hall opened into a living room, its lamps dimmed. The room was done in peach. A gray couch with peach flowers. Two peach settees. Over the fireplace, a huge still life of peaches. And on the coffee table, a bowl of frosted glass peaches. Talk about overkill.

Through its arched doorway they expected the kitchen but found instead another living room. And after that, yet another living room. Both were dimmed. One was in teal ("a terrible color," Alexis whispered), and the other in mauve ("possibly the worst color ever," smirked Helene). Of course, the mauve room sprouted silk lilacs and a still life with an eggplant and a magnifying glass, and in the teal room, teal ducks glided across the coffee table and into the oil paintings. Alexis, turning in circles to take everything in, gasped in awe of the grandeur. Sure it was hideous, but it took a lot of courage (not to mention a *lot* of money) to create such deluxe ugliness.

"Come *on*." Helene tugged at Alexis's sleeve. "Let's try this way." Alexis took her hand and followed her down another hallway, and for one second they felt like they were back in Camelot.

Camelot was the name of the kingdom the girls invented when they were ten, shortly after they'd met Madonna. It was inhabited only by queens (the girls themselves), princesses, horses, and one evil stepfather who lived on a yacht. Helene was Queen of the Princesses and Alexis was Queen of the Horses, and they ruled the land—which conveniently fit inside their living room—for a full two years. One day, in sixth grade,

Helene asked to play Camelot, and Alexis said, "Don't you know we're too old for pretend lands? Daddy's going to buy us real horses." And then the game was over. Alexis wasn't trying to be mean. She was just practical that way.

They each let the other's hand drop when the hallway opened up into a dining room. It was a stunning tribute to polo. An iron statue of a horse pranced as a centerpiece, and on two walls hung framed watercolors of polo players. "Sheer opulence," Helene said. "This family is filthy rich."

"You know," Alexis said, fiddling with the antique riding tack and saddle that rested on an end table. "They're not so different from us. You should realize that." Helene sometimes forgot that her mother had married Hugo Worth, one of the wealthiest men in America. Perhaps it was because she wasn't used to being wealthy. Alexis, on the other hand, was quite used to being rich, and she was always pointing out to Helene the ways their wealth wasn't something to be ashamed of. That is, if you used it responsibly. And if you decorated responsibly.

"No, Alexis. You don't get it. Look!" Helene said, pointing at a glimmering gold-green painting of a haystack covering one wall. "It's a real Monet. Look at the signature. And it matches the room!"

Alexis, so impressed she lost her voice, nodded her agreement. The Worths were rich. They were even rich, rich. But they weren't rich *rich* rich. Not like the Husseins.

The girls' stomachs were grumbling loud enough to wake the family, so thank God the kitchen was on the other side of the dining room. Only it was surprisingly bare. There was nothing on the walls except a few crayon drawings of lines and squiggles that must have been Richard originals—framed, of course. And there was little in the cupboard besides tins of biscuits. Helene picked up a tin of especially dry crackers and thought about her vow: low carbs in London. But what was she supposed to do? Starve?

Just as she pulled open the tin, a horrendous yelping began, and startled, she dropped the can of crackers. It clattered noisily against the metal shelf. Alexis was doubled over, laughing so hard she could only point. Under the kitchen table, on a round mattress embroidered with bones, was a dog. A poodle no less. It was not pleased at all to have been woken up, and it was headed for Helene's bare ankles.

Then they ran. They ran past horses and ducks, past lilacs and peaches, past rows and rows of blissfully silent poodles, Helenalexis, the MasterWorth Sisters, the two queens of Camelot. It was a blissfully innocent moment—but unfortunately it wasn't going to last.

When the girls heard someone banging around outside their room, they decided it was safe enough to leave again. They'd been dressed for hours, Alexis in hip-hugging jeans, a white button-down, pearls, and sling-backs, and Helene done up for her first day at work in pale blue cowboy boots, a pinstriped mini, a black hoodie, and a pink rhinestone belt. Alexis, carefully applying mascara, complimented Helene on perfectly matching her belt to her hair.

The clamor turned out to be Aunt Barbara dropping a brief-case and scattering files across the hall carpet. They crouched to help gather the papers, and she began chattering as soon as she saw them.

"I'm so sorry I won't have time this morning to show you around the place, such as it is; we're almost living in squalor these days. But I have a meeting, planning another benefit. This time for the orphans. The Chechen orphans. Poor dears. They're remarkably fruitful, benefits. Do you like them? Your mother does work for them, I'm sure. But do come to break-fast now. I'll sit for just one minute before I go."

Helene and Alexis were ushered to the kitchen by Aunt Barbara after she'd gathered all her papers. The dog began barking as soon as they entered. "Ohhh, little Mitsy-pooh," Aunt Barbara squealed. "She's my poodle-baby," she explained to the girls. "Have you met her?"

Helene stared at the refrigerator, and Alexis became very interested in her fingernails. If they looked at each other—or the dog—they'd lose it.

Breakfast consisted of toast and butter. For once Alexis ate more than Helene, who was too excited about her first day at the gallery to stop talking long enough to eat.

"I mean, it has everything, from da Vinci to Renoir to Turner. And lots of artists use the collection for inspiration. Who do you think I'll meet today? Lucian Freud? Damien Hirst? I hope I'm not too in awe to talk to them."

Alexis listened glumly. First of all, Helene was never too in awe to talk to anyone. Second of all, what was *she* supposed to do for ten hours while Helene met famous artists?

As if reading her mind, Aunt Barbara interrupted Helene to ask Alexis how she'd spend her days. "I assume you'll be at the shops. I mean, Helene's an artist and you love shopping. Isn't that correct?"

Nichola, who had her face buried in a magazine, snickered, and Alexis didn't think she was laughing at what she read. She glanced over though, just in case. The magazine in Nichola's hands was some garish punk-rock thing—much more up Helene's alley than Alexis's. What was the perfectly tartan-ensconced girl from the airport doing reading such a magazine? Not exactly *Vogue,* in other words. With a start, Alexis remembered the little story she'd made up on the flight to impress Tony.

"Lexy?" Aunt Barbara said.

But Alexis just smiled mysteriously and reached for another piece of toast.

"Oh, my god," Helene shrieked suddenly, jumping up from the table. "I have to go, or I'll be so late. See you. Love you." She ran out the door, leaving Alexis staring at the piece of toast in her hand, the mysterious, determined smile still playing on her face.

Ten hours later, a black cab dropped a tired Helene back at 46 Whittington Place in the posh Kensington district. She stayed outside to savor the moment: She was coming home from work for the first time! The Hussein house was large, white, and stately, on a block of other large, white, stately houses. Up and down the street, gardeners were trimming hedges in the setting sun, nannies were herding their broods in strollers home from Hyde Park, and black cabs let out impatient men in suits, each with the newspaper under his right arm.

Feeling understandably proud, Helene walked into the house and rushed into the bedroom to find Alexis. She planned to describe her day to her sister, beginning with the tour of the gallery, ending with her very own desk and phone and Filofax in a subterranean cinderblock office. She'd met the other interns (all British girls), but she hadn't met any famous painters. And the job they had her do—learning how to make a cup of British tea for the boss—wasn't *exactly* artistic. Still it was only the first day.

But Alexis wasn't in the bedroom. Nor was she in any of the living rooms. And she wasn't in the dining room where Barbara and Basha were running around setting the table. Each place had three forks and a stack of three plates arranged smallest to largest. "Saheed," Barbara whispered while adjusting the tulips in the vase, "is actually going to be home for dinner. This is an event. We will all sit down together in precisely twenty-three minutes."

Twenty-two minutes later Saheed arrived home, hungry and tired. Barbara had convinced Nichola to take off her shorts and tank top and put on a long black dress, and Helene felt herself ready to burst with news of her day. But Alexis was nowhere to be seen.

"There's absolutely nothing to be done about it," Barbara proclaimed. "We must eat immediately. It is time."

Despite the fineness of the china and Saheed's three-piece suit, despite the Monet painting shimmering on the wall and the care with which Basha placed each item on their plates, the food sucked. There was no other way to describe it. The soup managed to be both watery and clogged with stringy meat. The salad swam in oil. And the meat pie was, well, a meat pie (Helene didn't even *want* to know what the meat was, due to a certain joke Hugo had made about steak-and-kidney pie shortly before the girls left). Helene thought about announcing her commitment to vegetarianism, but she never got a chance to; through the first three courses, Aunt Barbara held forth nonstop on her latest accomplishment on the charity circuits. "The orphan benefit will have entertainment from an orphaned boys' choir! We arranged for a conductor to begin working at the orphanage, teaching the boys how to sing in chorus, and what do you know? These children are gifted! Well, except for one poor soul who sings dreadfully out of key and can be heard above the rest—he rather reminds me of a balloon losing its air, but that's no matter. It's the work and effort that count. And we're putting him in the back away from the mikes."

And on and on until Helene started to despair that anyone would notice the change in her. How she sat in her chair with the posture of a young woman with a job. How she crooked her pinkie like a woman with responsibilities. Thankfully, as Basha cleared the meat pie, Saheed interrupted Barbara. "Dear, your orphan bash sounds enthralling. But I think that our niece just had her first day at work. Helene, how did it go?"

"Well," Helene began, suddenly unsure how to present the momentum of her day. It felt huge, but nothing had really happened. "I have now seen all the back rooms of the National Gallery and—"

Just then Alexis stormed in, carrying a Selfridges bag in each arm. "I'm so sorry I'm late," she said, tossing her bags against the wall and taking a seat. Her face was as calm and serene as ever. She looked neither apologetic nor in a rush.

"Alexis," Helene reprimanded, "have you been shopping all this time?"

Alexis's eyes went wide as a doll's. "Shopping? Oh, those bags. They're nothing. It's just that I was told to wear a British designer for my first day at work, and all I brought with me was Michael Kors and Marc Jacobs."

"Work?" asked Barbara, Saheed, and Helene all at once.

Alexis stirred the soup that Basha had placed in front of her. She tried not to smile, but her face lit up despite herself. It was perfectly glowing. "I sort of got a job," she said, still staring at her soup. "Just an internship really. With *Vogue*. British *Vogue*."

"With *who*?" Helene asked. She was amazed and a tad annoyed. She wanted to be happy for Alexis. After all, weren't best friends always happy for each other? But tonight the attention was supposed to be focused on Helene. It had been her first day at work. She was the one who'd won the prestigious internship that brought them to London.

"British *Vogue*. You know, Stella McCartney, Alexander McQueen, John Galliano."

"Oh!" Barbara squealed. "All my favorites. You'll have to introduce me, or at least give me a sneak preview of the winter lines."

"Well, this deserves a toast," Saheed exclaimed in his deep, imperial voice. "Basha, open the Riesling I've been saving and bring some sparkling water for the girls."

Even Nichola said, "Congratulations," and her normally cynical eyes widened with admiration.

"Today I sat in on the editorial meeting for the September issue. They were debating whether to do a photo spread of actors under thirty or actors over thirty. Of course, I think they should do one of the royal family, but I didn't say anything." She winked at Helene.

Suddenly it all came back to Helene. The plane ride. Milk shakes. The photo of William (*her* William). The bet. Helene realized that her guarded feelings toward Alexis had been growing since yesterday's plane trip when Alexis showed interest in Prince William. The two sisters were supposed to do different things. That was the unspoken rule of their friendship. Alexis had the grace and elegance; she had the ballet-dancer body and the sleek, fashionable clothes. Every guy in school mooned over her. Helene brought in the grades; she held the giant sleepovers. She was the reason the house got rolled with toilet paper by the football team. She was everyone's friend and confidante. She was intense and creative and had nailed a summer internship. And she used to have a private little crush on Prince William that was all her own.

Now Alexis was breaking the implicit separate-but-equal code. She was trespassing.

Helene willed herself to find some generosity for her sister as the meal dragged on. But it was hard because Alexis was still talking about her new job. Wasn't she supposed to be the shy one?

Alexis explained how she landed the interview. On a whim she'd decided to walk by the offices of *Vogue*. She'd been standing outside awhile, just admiring the tall glass doors, when a girl ran out sobbing. Alexis offered her a tissue and asked her what was wrong. It turned out that this girl was an intern and her boss was none other than the erratic and impetuous Lady Brawn, British *Vogue*'s editor-in-chief. While bawling, the girl described how Lady Brawn had yelled at her that morning because her latte wasn't foamy enough and the dry cleaning was late. She fired the poor girl on the spot. As soon as the former intern walked away sniffling, Alexis thought, *What would Helene do if she were in this situation?* Then, fortified, she opened the tall glass doors, smiled at the receptionist, and marched into the editor-in-chief's office. What did she have to lose?

"I'm Alexis Worth," she'd said, extending her hand to a shocked Lady Brawn. "I'd like to be your new intern. Tell me what you'd like me to accomplish first."

And just like that, she was hired, and soon she was sitting in on her first editorial meeting.

As Helene listened to Alexis's recounting of her day, she thought about the hours she had spent writing and rewriting the application for her internship. She thought about the hours of studying artists and their masterpieces. She thought about how it all had culminated in her learning to make the perfect cup of English tea. And then she decided not to think anymore. She decided to be happy for her lovely sister, who had taken a job working for a monster. Helene resolved to borrow a page from Alexis's book and make sure she did everything as perfectly as possible at her new internship. Then maybe they'd trust her to do more than make tea. Then maybe they'd send her to the Royal Ball, where Helene would meet her prince. It would all be fine. So why was she still so supremely jealous of Alexis?

"I'm so happy for you, Alexis," Helene said, trying to hold back her tears. Then she ran out of the room.

5

Working Nine to Five

TO A BUDDING artist in love with Prince William, nothing could sound more magical than the Royal Ball at the National Gallery. It turned out that nothing was as boring as preparation for this event, an event she wasn't even sure she could go to. Helene spent her first week at the gallery dealing with a mountain of envelopes. First, the invitations needed to be folded. "Remember," reprimanded stern Ms. Ming, her supervisor, "be sure to align the gold ribbons perfectly." After six hours of such folding, Helene's back and shoulders ached, and forgetting her vow to do everything as perfectly as Alexis, Helene found herself shoving misfolded invites into envelopes when Ms. Ming wasn't looking.

The next day, the envelopes needed to be labeled. "Each label must form a ninety-degree angle with the floral decoration on the envelope," reminded Ms. Ming.

On Thursday, Helene sealed each envelope. No licking: Helene had to dip a small sponge in a bowl of water and swipe it across the glued surface. On Friday, joy of joys, Helene was sent to the post office, where the line stretched around the block. She put on her iPod and breathed in the fresh, non-basement air.

At night she dreamed of stacks of envelopes, their mouths menacingly flapping open and closed. Like the rest of the staff, Helene entered and left by a side entrance, and hadn't gone into the actual art galleries since her orientation. So it hardly felt like she was working in the art world at all. She always brought her sketch book, thinking she would stay late and sketch, but by the time Ms. Ming released her, she stumbled home on the Tube, too tired to take in the glamour of London.

Alexis also collapsed at the end of each day, but not out of the tedium of her job. Hardly. She spent the first day shadowing the stylist on a photo shoot at Trafalgar Square. On Tuesday, she sampled lipsticks for an article called "Shades of Scarlet." Wednesday found her calling Stella McCartney's press agent to fact-check a story on Stella's handbags. And on Thursday, long-legged Alexis was dolled up in a peasant dress and told to lie on her stomach in the background of a photo shoot. A real photo shoot!

"They just needed someone in the background to make the people in the foreground stand out," Alexis explained to Helene. But her modesty couldn't mask the truth: Alexis's photo would be in *Vogue*! Thankfully, Helene was too tired and amazed to muster up any jealousy. Besides, she told herself, she would have hated to work with all those models. She needed substance. She needed depth. Dismally, she wondered if a basement office counted as depth.

On Saturday morning, Helene packed her sketch pad and pencils in her backpack. Relieved to be out of work clothes, she slipped on her Pumas and a green shirt that proclaimed, VIRGINIA

IS FOR LOVERS. (When David, her best friend, pointed out that certain practices were illegal in Virginia, she'd crossed out "Lovers" with a red Magic Marker and written "Losers" over it.) She reminded herself she must find a witty postcard to send him.

"I am going to the Tate Modern to sketch. Will you come?" she asked Alexis.

Alexis, who was blow-drying her hair even straighter, didn't hear. But noticing that Helene was talking to her, she nodded anyway. Since working at *Vogue,* she'd become even more style-conscious, if that was possible. Eschewing her three suitcases of American clothes, she now dressed head to toe in British designers. Lunch had become a distant, Scarsdale memory. She was even thinking about taking up smoking, but it was just too gross for her to do more than contemplate it. When the girls got outside, Helene pulled a Tube map from her backpack and sat on the sidewalk to decipher it.

"Since this is Kensington, we'll take the line to Waterloo Station. Then we can walk along the Thames before ending up at the Tate Modern."

"The Tate?" Alexis said. "Who said anything about the Tate? I thought we were going shopping!" Alexis walked in front of a suited businessman and stuck out her arm for a cab like a seasoned New Yorker.

"But Alexis," Helene said, joining her sister after apologizing to the businessman for their rudeness, "it's totally easy to get to the museum on the Tube. I love riding the Tube. And the Tate! They've got some great exhibitions going on."

"Oh, Helene, you spend every day in a museum. Don't you want to see something truly beautiful?"

"Like what?"

"Clothes, of course. All the lovely clothes at Harrods."

Just then a rounded black cab pulled up in front of them. Alexis opened the door and said, "To Harrods, please." Helene had no choice but to shove her Tube map into her pocket and join her stepsister.

Not that it was so bad. After all, if department stores were paintings, Harrods would be the *Mona Lisa*. If department stores were food, Harrods would be caviar (which was gross, because it was fish eggs, but good because it was expensive and rare).

And, Helene reasoned, these days all famous artists dressed exquisitely. Fashion, she figured, was just a lesser art form that she would have to dabble in. And maybe Alexis would give her a few tips. As she was reminded every single time she addressed, stuffed, and sealed an invitation, the Royal Ball at the National Gallery was fast approaching.

6

♛

Bird Watching

SUMMER VACATION IN London meant one thing to boys finishing Eton: birds. No, not the kind that fly overhead or crap on your sleeve or appear in a McNugget. But chicks, honeys, girls, birds. And what better place to spot birds than in their natural habitat, the department store?

Eton is the most prestigious public school in England. And by public school, the Brits mean private school. Eton's full of the best and brightest young lads—well, at least the richest plus the supersmart kids on scholarship. It offers them everything: gorgeous grounds, horses to ride, the finest teachers, pubs that serve underage. Everything, that is, except girls.

"Mums are hot," Laszlo said. He was reclining on a massage chair by the escalator in the Home department at Harrods. They'd already been kicked out of Junior Collections for loitering and shooed away from Lingerie after it was clear they were not, in fact, lingerie reporters for the *Guardian* newspaper. So the Home department was all that was left to Laszlo and Simon, recent Eton graduates. And Housewares was cluttered with mothers. Or mums.

Simon, sitting next to Laszlo, rested his head in his palm to seriously consider that proclamation. "Mums. Well, a certain type, definitely. But not all of them as a category. I'd venture there's a subcategory of hot mums. They're young and they have one kid only. And . . . well, what does it matter? You can't have them."

"Why not?" asked Laszlo incredulously, as he waved at a mother attempting to push a stroller up the escalator despite the posted warning against doing precisely that.

"They're married," Simon said.

"Oh, whatever. Besides, your mum's not married anymore."

"Don't you dare say that my mum's hot."

"Fine, she's not hot."

"You idiot. You can't say that either."

"I'm not trying to say anything about her hotness, my dear friend. I'm *trying* to say that the problem with mums is not their marital status. It's that they're dull. Look at the blonde on the escalator. All that attention to the baby. None to me. It's a dismal proposition. I'd rather snog a chair." At that, Laszlo turned the massager up to ten and started an exaggerated gyration of ecstasy. "Ohhh," he moaned, as his chair quickly pulsed from the top of his head down to his tailbone. "Ohhhh!"

Simon and Laszlo had been housemates and fast friends for four years despite their obvious differences. Simon was quiet and rather passive when it came to girls; Laszlo was a clown. Simon's parents were well-heeled Londoners, with some distant connection to the royal family. Laszlo was a genuine royal. That is, he was about ten times removed from the Czech monarchy. His parents had moved from the Czech Republic when Laszlo was four and found jobs cleaning flats (apartments) and fixing flats (tires). He'd attended Eton as a King's Scholar, which is a nice way of saying a scholarship kid. Maybe because of the incongruity between his home and school, he found British stuffiness absolutely ridiculous and loved mocking it. "Uhhh, uhhh," he sighed.

"Look, Laszlo, could you just stop it?" Simon began. "I mean, I get the joke, ha-ha, but tone it down maybe just a bit."

Laszlo groaned all the more loudly.

Simon gave up. He perched on the edge of his recliner with his legs crossed and looked toward a display of lamps, trying to give the impression of someone who just happened to be sitting next to this most unfortunate person, someone who was perhaps a bit fatigued and whose girlfriend was still shopping. He was busy picturing this fantasy girlfriend—what she looked like, what she was shopping for—when Laszlo screamed, *"Yeeeowww!"* Apparently the massage chair had blown some sort of circuit and was smoking something terrible. Laszlo let loose some rather terrible words as he leaped from his seat.

The mums to which the boys had been referring now cast Laszlo and Simon dirty looks as they hurried their kids in the opposite direction. Just then, Simon saw two young women walking from the lamp display straight toward them. He cleared his throat and tried to reason with Laszlo once more: "Shh, they work here and they're going to kick us out if you don't stop. Then how will we meet anyone?"

But the two people headed toward them weren't the girls who spritzed perfume as you walked by, or the girls who gift-wrapped, or the girls who offered free makeovers. One was a pretty, punky girl with blond hair accented with a bright streak of pink, who was nearly doubled over with hysterics, and the girl next to her was a gorgeous brunette carrying three olive and gold Harrods shopping bags. This girl stared fiercely at the escalators and said in that drawn-out American way, "Oh, god, what a freak. Let's go." She looked as mortified as Simon felt, and when she caught his eye, Simon couldn't help it: He smiled.

Alexis grinned back and then immediately regretted it. The boy may have been handsome in that tall, thin, pretty-boy way, but his friend was a nightmare. And she and Helene hadn't yet visited floors four or five: stationery, pens, and leather goods. "Helene," she whispered, "come *on*." But it was too late. Pretty Boy had already stood up, apologized profusely for his friend, and held out his hand.

"I'm Simon," he said, in an accent that could make any American girl's heart jump. "Lovely to meet you." Alexis reached out her hand in return. She was always gracious to a boy with a beautiful voice. His face wasn't offending anyone either.

His friend, who was busily throwing towels onto the smoking chair, stopped and turned his attention to the group. "I Laszlo," he said. "How you do? You being well? I meet you, yes?" Alexis had a flash of concern that she'd been mocking someone with a learning disability, or a language barrier, but when she zeroed in on his calm face and sparkling eyes, she knew she and her sister were being duped.

Helene, her gullible sister, was not so perceptive.

"I'm Helene," she said earnestly. "Are you from Mexico?"

"My country," he said, "is no Mexico. I no being Mexico. My country far, far from here. Very good country. Country have beautiful women, no? Like you? You beautiful women be coming to my country and me, yes?"

Alexis thought about all the clothes lying patiently on their hangers while this boy prattled on. It was a shame. "Extremely nice to meet you, Laszlo," she said sarcastically, "but we're late."

"Late for what?" Helene asked.

"Plan B," Alexis whispered.

"Just a sec," Helene whispered back. This wasn't an emergency. This was just your basic flirting. And besides, Alexis had been going on all day about what it had been like to have a makeup artist do her face for her *Vogue* photo shoot. It was Helene's turn to shine.

"Look," Simon said, trying desperately not to stare too long at Alexis, "you'll have to pardon Laszlo—"

"Many beautiful women. Many, many beautiful women," Laszlo was saying. "Your country being America, no? I hear it in your vase."

"That's 'voice,' Laszlo. Now, really, just ignore him. He's from the Czech Republic, you know, and his English is limited." Simon was playing along reluctantly, out of habit, out of his perpetual passivity. He used to find it hilarious when Laszlo, who had perfectly refined manners and poise, assumed the role of pervy foreigner. But did he *have* to do it in front of these two particularly lovely girls?

"Excuse, but I help needed."

"Well, what kind of help?" Helene asked, her sweet face furrowed with concern, as Alexis transferred all her bags to her left hand and tugged her sister toward the escalator.

"Help to making the love," Laszlo said, kissing the air, as if unaware of his mistake in syntax.

Eyes wide, cheeks burning, Helene turned to her sister. "Plan B," she said. *"Now."*

Simon punched Laszlo hard on the arm just as the girls lifted into the air—*like angels,* Simon thought—on the escalator. Laszlo immediately regretted his behavior; as usual, he was too late. He really, truly wanted to meet a girl, someone to talk to, to kiss. But girls intimidated him, especially pretty Americans with pink hair and so . . .

"You made a fool of yourself," Simon said. "I'm getting tired of it, Laz."

Then, in an uncharacteristically forward move, Simon ran up the escalator, pushing mothers and babies out of his way. "Wait," he screamed. "He's a real wanker! He was just joking."

At the top, Alexis and Helene found themselves trapped. Pretty Boy was overtaking them, yet the floor they'd reached was swamped with teenagers. They saw no other option than to step onto the down escalator, with Simon following close behind. Laszlo, seeing an opportunity to redeem himself, sprinted up the down escalator, further infuriating every single Harrods shopper. When he reached the girls, he bowed and said gallantly, "I was kidding. I speak English. Really I do. And I have never kissed a girl. Don't plan to. Don't think I'd like it at all."

Simon, out of breath, reached the step behind them. "You both seem very nice. As a rule, Americans are dying to see the tourist spots, and it just so happens that we're on our way to Piccadilly Circus. Won't you come?"

Alexis's resolve melted when he spoke. He sounded exactly like Hugh Grant. She turned to Helene. "Plan C?" she asked.

7

Authentic Experiences

"IT'S A FINE idea in theory, but you have to admit that in practice it's a bit damp," Simon said. Helene had insisted they sit on the top floor of the open-topped double-decker bus. She wanted to experience as much of London as possible now that she had a day off. But this being London, the meager sun had been subsumed by a swath of deep purple cloud, and it had begun to rain. Pour, rather. The girls hadn't even thought to bring umbrellas.

"No umbrellas?" Laszlo asked in horror. "But this is England. An umbrella is as essential as water. Or rather, an umbrella is essential because of water."

"Well, where are *your* umbrellas?" asked Alexis, trying to keep her packages dry by shoving them under the seat. She wanted to stay with the boys, but she also wanted to protect her new suede skirt—folded in tissue inside her purse—from the ruinous rain.

"We're blokes," said Laszlo. "Rain only makes us stronger."

"Or rather, we know better than to ever go outside. Come on. Let's go somewhere warm and have a pint," Simon said, gathering Alexis's bags.

"But we've only gone one block on the bus," Helene complained. "It's an authentic London experience!"

"Helene, you can have your English experience when you buy an umbrella," Simon said in a motherly reprimand. "Till then, it's off to the pub with you."

They ran into the first open door they found. It turned out to be a Starbucks, with exactly the same green-uniformed servers and photos of coffee beans in various stages of roasting as at the Starbucks on Boston Post Road in Mamaroneck. Simon brought four espressos to the table. "Here's to London!"

They dispensed with the specifics right away. The girls learned that Simon and Laszlo were eighteen, just done with Eton, and off to Oxford and Cambridge, respectively. The boys learned about the fortuitous romance of Hugo Worth and Brenda Masterson, the fabulous summer internships, and the hallway of poodle paintings at Aunt Barbara's house.

"Aunt Barbara's current obsession seems to be Chechen orphans," Helene said, smiling.

"Is she going to collect photos of them to line a new room?" Laszlo asked.

"Maps of the Balkans on the wall," Helene added. "A statue of a child as a centerpiece."

Suddenly worried that she and Helene were being insensitive, Alexis asked bluntly, "What about your families?"

"Royal," Laszlo said. Alexis, quickly remembering the bet, gasped and leaned forward in her seat. "Do you mean that as an adjective or a noun? Like are they royal, as in cool? Or royal as in royalty?"

"Well," Simon began, "my father is, uh, employed by the

royal family—by Her Majesty the Queen, if you must. And Laszlo—"

"I have royal blood in me. Almost enough to fill my right thumb. Although I might have gotten rid of it in my last donation of blood for the war effort. I'm related to the now-deposed monarchy, but then so was about half the country. It's great, because it means my parents are dirt-poor immigrants."

"Well, at least you went to Eton," said Alexis, thinking practically.

Helene laughed. "I think your life sounds fascinating. Where we live—Westchester County in New York—driving a Toyota counts as poverty. I plan on broadening my knowledge while I'm here." She said this with great satisfaction. She glanced at Laszlo. She didn't know what to make of him. He looked almost like a man, definitely more grown up than her friends. He had wide shoulders and a round face with cheekbones that angled out like wings. His eyes were the palest blue, nearly gray, the down of a bird, and his forehead was clear as porcelain. And at times he seemed calm and assured. But more often he acted like a smart-aleck fourteen-year-old. He was constantly moving, jiggling his leg or stacking the red stirrers or unscrewing the sugar container so its contents would spill out if someone tried to use it. He seemed at odds with himself.

Not Simon. Simon, Helene figured, was the most authentically English thing she'd seen that day. Everything about him was equal parts proper and slouchy. His dark hair was tousled in a faux Mohawk, his blue oxford shirt was torn on one sleeve, and the laces of his Campers were undone. Just the kind of dishevelment that smacks of wealth. She wondered what exactly his father did for the queen, and glancing at Alexis, who was telling him about her skill at jumping fences while sitting on a horse, Helene could see that her sister wondered the same.

Just then an American family wearing matching We Escaped the Tower of London T-shirts walked in and started shouting, "One decaf, double cap with skim milk."

"One iced chai latte, one frappuccino, extra caramel syrup."

"Da-ad, tell them I want extra caramel syrup. Extra syrup!"

"Are you sure you're American?" Laszlo asked. "Because it seems as if all Americans scream. Come on, scream unpleasantly."

"It's ridiculous that this is all you're seeing of London," said Simon, gathering their empty cups. "Here." He handed them each a section of newspaper to cover their heads and grabbed Alexis's bags. "Follow me."

Simon led them to the Brazen Head Pub, which was much more like it, if by "it" you mean bottle-glass windows, dark wooden tables, a barmaid who calls you "luv," and Guinness on tap. Laszlo showed Helene how to lose pound after pound (money, unfortunately, not weight) on a fruit machine—a pinball-looking lottery game that, according to Laszlo, you had to be either a genius or a professional alcoholic to figure out. Alexis and Helene ordered Red Bulls and took it all in. Alexis talked about horses with Simon, discussed the latest on the Olsen twins with Laszlo, and laughed and laughed with Helene. Usually her days were a series of goals. There was something she wanted, so she worked to get it. Then she moved on to the next item on the list she kept in her head. But since she'd arrived in London, she'd felt free of all that. It was like the feeling she got riding a Ferris wheel. Whatever she wanted was somewhere on the ground, but she was too distracted by the pretty passing lights to care. Very unlike Alexis Worth.

Helene, who always had an easier time having fun, was now forcing Laszlo to put Milli Vanilli on the jukebox and was trying to convince him that the new American dance craze was the electric slide. Alexis smiled and admired her sister; while she herself took great pains to *look* like someone who felt free, Helene just was. But Alexis could tell that something was missing from Helene's normal joie de vivre. Her eyes weren't shining as they always did. Alexis had the feeling it had to do with their little bet, and she couldn't understand it. She would never admit it to Helene, but if Prince William walked into this pub right now, he'd without a doubt choose Helene over Alexis. That was a fact.

Noticing how distracted Alexis was by what he thought was her thoughtful staring at Laszlo, Simon worried he was boring her. There was something about Laszlo that he didn't have. A certain carelessness. Sure Laszlo could be a total goof and overcompensate for whatever shyness he had, but in the end the girls always laughed. With his delicate looks and runner's body, Simon didn't seem like the kind of guy who would be insecure around girls. And he'd had girlfriends before, but Eton made it so annoyingly difficult. You got to know someone over the summer, and she sent you a letter or photo every day in September, but by Christmas she'd moved on. His mother called him a catch. His father, when he was around, told him to skip all of the in-between stuff and go straight for home base. His aunts dubbed him the Heartbreaker. So why did he feel like he'd spent his whole life waiting for a real girlfriend?

"I know," he said too loudly, nearly knocking over his pint trying to get Alexis to look at him again. "Let's do something totally touristy and cheesy and buy T-shirts. Big Ben or the Tower or Madame Tussaud's."

"That's it," Alexis said, her cheeks flushed now from the sudden warmth of the room. She was thankful to Simon for interrupting her worries. She hated to feel anxiety about this stupid competition; she should be having fun. "I've always wanted to go to Madame Tussaud's. Imagine, all my favorite people in one place."

8

♛

Waxing Poetic

BRITNEY SPEARS. MADONNA. Cher. James Dean. Arnold Schwarzenegger. Kylie. Each one required oohing and aahing, tempered by a good deal of wisecracking. It was possible that they made Britney's butt too small. Tom Cruise's nose was less crooked. Madonna's arms were actually more muscular in person (the girls spoke from authority on this point). Alexis wanted a photo with Posh Spice; Helene wanted one with Nelson Mandela. Out in the faux English countryside, Arnold Schwarzenegger dined with Jean Paul Gaultier, and inside on a spiral staircase leading to a ballroom, Saddam Hussein saluted in the general direction of George and Laura Bush.

The four nonwax kids had kept together as they toured the museum, but in the Great Hall they were separated by throngs of tourists. It was like Grand Central Station at rush hour. Laszlo found himself squashed against John Lennon as a swarm of Japanese schoolchildren snapped their cameras. He made a fine fifth Beatle, if he did say so himself. Simon had been requisitioned by two German women to take their picture with the seven-foot-tall muscle-bound Rock. And Helene wandered aimlessly, pretending she was at a gala party thrown by the queen with all of the world's leaders and tyrants—she'd decided the tourists were servants and butlers. She couldn't pause too long in any spot, however, or the illusion would quickly be broken by flashlights and American accents.

"Helene! Over here." Helene looked around to find the source of Alexis's call. The girls hadn't had a minute alone since they met the boys in Harrods, and they needed to hash it all out: Which one was cuter? Was Laszlo too weird? But weren't they nice showing them around? Nicer than American guys by far.

Alexis clearly had something else on her mind. "Look," she said, pointing to a stage near the spiral staircase. Helene followed her finger to find a montage of royal proportions. Literally. The queen, sprightly and well-coiffed, stood with Prince Charles and Princess Diana behind her. Off to the side, looking a little embarrassed to be standing up in front of everyone, were William and his punchy brother Harry.

William winked.

"Oh," Helene said, as longing clenched her heart, and her crush came back like a wave crashing on top of her. Maybe, just maybe, she could get Alexis to forget the bet. "Cool," she said, as calmly as she could. "It's the royal family. Let's go find the guys."

No such luck. Alexis grabbed Helene's arm and whispered, "I figured out something important. Simon and Laszlo went to Eton, right? They probably know him."

Helene stared at her sister blankly. But inside she felt a growing terror.

"Don't you get it?" Alexis said. "If we play our cards right, they can introduce us to him."

What frightened Helene was the complete lack of anxiety in Alexis's voice. Helene knew who the mannequin on the stage would choose if he suddenly came to life.

"Come on, Alexis. The bet was just a joke." Helene tried not to catch William's eye, instead focusing on a little boy trying to put his cotton candy up the nose of Al Pacino. It was possible that she could stand not winning William—as long as her sister didn't get him either.

"A joke? The joke'll be on you when you're calling me Your Highness."

For Alexis everything was very clear. She was enjoying herself. But this flirting for the fun of it would get old. The summer had to have a purpose, and *Vogue* was one part of it—and their William contest was the other. One must have a goal in order to have something to work toward. It was now clear to Alexis, even if it wasn't to Helene, why they'd followed the boys: to catch their prince. *Her* prince.

For a few minutes neither girl spoke. They simply gazed at the stage.

Alexis saw herself done up in wax, next to her husband, the prince. She'd be wearing a Versace gown. No, not elegant enough. Oscar de la Renta. Or perhaps Carolina Herrera. Or maybe, her eyes scanning the room, she'd be daring and wear Gaultier. She'd be the rebel princess, fusing fashion with courtly duties. Helene, on the other hand, saw only William. First he smiled that slow, crooked smile at her. Then he opened his mouth and said, *It's nice to see you in London.*

"It's nice to see you too," Helene mouthed.

Then why aren't you smiling?

"It's Alexis. I hate to compete against her. We shouldn't. We're best friends."

Competition isn't evil. It's just about going after what you want. That is, if you want it. Do you want it, Helene? William's smile grew even brighter. *Do you want* me*?*

"Helene," Alexis said, interrupting her stepsister's daydream, "were you just talking to the wax figure of William?"

"Actually, I was just about to say that you should be thinking of what to wear when you join me for tea at the palace. Don't worry, I'll make sure not to invite you on the same day as Leo. I wouldn't want to pour salt in your wounds."

Alexis laughed. She was relieved to see Helene enjoying the fight. "Actually, I was just thinking that when you call me Your Highness, you'll have to do a little curtsy. Better practice in those microminis."

"As if," said Helene, who spent almost every nonworking day in jeans.

"Nice hat on the Queen Mum, don't you think?" asked Simon.

The girls swung around to see the boys standing behind them.

"Do you know him?" she fired off in the Alexis voice that demanded obedience. Unless, apparently, you were Laszlo.

"Never met the guy," he said, staring at Simon. "Don't know why he's been hanging around us all day. Sir, could you leave now? Sir? Please don't make me call security."

"No, not him," Alexis said, gesturing toward the stage. *"Him."*

"Oh, sure," Laszlo said. "Old Willie. Bill. Billyboy. Best friend of mine, you know. I called him Will-ster, but that's just between pals. Sometimes, the Will-loosener. Bonny Prince Billy. Billabong, when he was being naughty. Oh, no. Oh, don't tell me! You find him dreamy!"

"You're always kidding around," Alexis said. Laszlo shrugged.

"Of course we know him," Simon said. "He was in our house at Eton a few years above us. But he's a, um, very private person, you know." He'd begun to think Alexis would never be interested in him. "Come here," he said, reaching for her hand. "I want to show you what you'll look like when they make your statue."

Alexis giggled and followed, leaving Laszlo and Helene to raid the gift shop for tacky T-shirts that proclaimed, Just the Wax, Please.

An hour later four tired teenagers went home. Two to Kensington. One to Hampstead. And one all the way on the Tube to South London. During his ride, Laszlo was thinking how lucky he and Simon were. Their first day cruising and they'd met the prettiest girls in all of England. And they were American, no less. Simon was thinking particularly of Alexis, how her arms and collarbone looked so fragile, but her blue eyes were fierce, a mesmerizing combination. He even allowed himself to believe that there was no way she could prefer clowning Laszlo to him. But did she? Was she thinking of him right then?

But the girls, yawning in the backseat of a cab, were thinking of another guy altogether. An old Etonian, yes, but not Simon or Laszlo. Helene still worried that she had no chance where Alexis was involved, but she would try for William. Alexis had no such concerns. The summer was shaping up to be the best ever. The girls had the coolest internships. They'd met two cute guys to pave their way to the prince. They'd have a summer of smooth sailing after all, even in a land so horribly damp and chilly. She hugged her Harrods bags close, then brushed back Helene's curls. Her sister had fallen asleep on her shoulder, and she looked like a painting. What was that artist's name? Bottachele? Bottacela? She'd ask Helene when she woke.

9

Naughty Nichola

BY THE END of Helene and Alexis's first Sunday in London, everything had become much, much more complicated. The morning had started out normally enough: The daily drizzle had turned into a downpour, and even Helene didn't try too hard to get them to a museum. While they waited for London to become less soggy, Helene sprawled out on the peach couch and returned to *Wuthering Heights*. Alexis was giving herself a pedicure in the bathroom.

After a few hours, Helene had once again put down *Wuthering Heights* and picked up a *Heat* she found lying on a side table. Unfortunately it didn't have any pictures of her prince, but there was a gossip item:

> *Just back from a month in Chile, helping build houses for the poor (aw, what a do-gooder), William has been spotted several times enjoying his summer vacation from college. Each time, naughty boy, he's been seen with a different girl*

(tsk, tsk). But all three of them have been tall, exquisitely thin, with the classic good looks royalty love. And rich. Oh, how rich they are! One was an heiress to the Gobstopper fortune. The second, a runway model and daughter of a CEO. The third was a well-known trust-fund party girl. Guess our William has a type! Ladies, you better hope you're it.

Helene wished desperately that she hadn't eaten that third piece of toast for breakfast. She felt her belly and thought that it must have expanded since she'd arrived in London. If she didn't eat any lunch, that would be a start. After all, she would never be tall. And she didn't think William, who had been building houses for the poor, really cared whether she was rich. After all, that's not why she liked him. But she could be thinner. She was sucking in her stomach when Aunt Barbara barged in.

"There you are, Helene dear." Barbara looked as stylish and frazzled as usual. She was wearing a short turquoise suit with narrow turquoise heels (her love of matching apparently extended to her outfits), and she carried both a comb and an egg salad sandwich. Helene worried she'd put the wrong one in her hair. "I was hoping I could ask a favor of you and Alexis today. Would you take Nichola out for the afternoon? She's been sulking in her room for the last few weeks, God knows what about, but I know she'd be tickled if her older cousins paid her some attention. I have to go to a luncheon and a trillion meetings, or I'd play with her myself. But in any case, you two are loads more fun."

Helene agreed, and closed the magazine on her lap with a sigh of relief. Nichola had been almost invisible since they'd returned from the airport, and Helene wanted to get to know her. But she worried that Alexis would be annoyed to have Nichola tagging along.

"Oh, and another thing, Helene," Barbara said as she left the room, the scent of Chanel No. 5 hovering behind her, "this is the formal living room. If you want to slouch around, please try the third living room down. But I do approve of your reading habits. If you could just get Nichola to pick up Brontë. Or any book. Any book at all." Helene tried to hide *Heat* under a couch pillow.

As Barbara left, Alexis walked in saying that she didn't care if it rained or sleeted or hailed. They just *had* to get out of the house. She would even go to any museum Helene wanted. When Helene told her sister of their new afternoon plans, Alexis looked pleased. "She's a cute girl," she said. "I was hoping she'd hang out with us more. She's always off on her own. I feel sad that she doesn't have any sisters. I'd have probably been that mopey and shy and secretive if you hadn't moved in."

Helene felt reassured by Alexis's generosity; it was exactly why they were so close from the beginning of their friendship. Because it didn't matter who got the internship or the prince. What mattered is that they had each other. *Wait a second, Helene,* she thought, as Alexis ran off to change her outfit— again. While it did matter that they had each other, it also mattered a great deal who got William. It mattered more than anything else this summer. The tricky part was getting William and keeping Alexis as her best friend. Helene realized that was shaping up to be the summer's biggest challenge.

According to Lady Brawn, who had been generous with her gossip, Prince William once liked conservatively dressed girls. No problem there: Alexis had brought preppy to Scarsdale High before anyone knew that it was back in style. "But," Lady Brawn whispered, "these days Will enjoyed 'a bit of vampish glamour.'" This was not Alexis's forte, but she was resourceful when it came to fashion, and she'd bought a few choice items at Harrods the day before. Now she pulled on a new tight black cashmere short-sleeved sweater, paired it with a black pencil skirt with a high slit, then added fishnets and knee-high black boots. Rummaging through Helene's backpack, she found the perfect red lipstick. It was called Gash, and it made her lips stand out like rose petals on her pale face.

She joined the others in the kitchen. Barbara and Helene were sitting at the round table, nibbling at a muffin. Nichola wasn't there yet, but her voice was: "You can't make me wear that stupid, ugly outfit!" she yelled from her room. "I don't care if you bought it in Selfridges or Marks and Spencer! You don't control me! I'm a free human, you know! And I know how to dress myself, far better than you've ever known!"

The girls, whose successful implementation of Plan B had made temper tantrums a thing of distant memory, now looked at each other with a combination of horror and admiration.

"But darling," Barbara called back, looking nervously at Alexis, then at Helene. "The outfit is lovely. Laura Ashley. It's very fashionable. And very smart. Right, Alexis? You know fashion. Isn't Laura Ashley smart? I just don't think girls your age should be wearing such short skirts. Besides," she said with a determined nod, "you'll catch your death of cold."

"You don't know anything, do you?" Nichola asked as she walked into the kitchen, causing even Helene and Alexis to gasp. Gone was the girl at the airport in a plaid jumper and ribbon. Nichola wore a black leather skirt that barely covered her underwear. Her white, ribbed tank top came to just beneath her considerable breasts. And she wavered on inch-high platform shoes. The look was Britney, but the posture was puberty: She crossed her arms protectively in front of her exposed midriff and hunched her shoulders to make her chest appear smaller.

"Oh, please take off that skirt this instant."

Nichola snorted and rolled her eyes. "All right. Here, though? You want me to take it off here and go out in my knickers?"

"You *know* what I mean, Nichola," Barbara pleaded. Alexis and Helene stared at their fingers on the table. This is why you need a sister—someone to stop you when you've gone too far.

"Maybe I do. But what do *you* know?" Nichola started circling the table where Alexis, Helene, and Barbara sat, and they followed her movements like spectators at an ice rink. Her shoes were so high that with each step she took it seemed she could fall flat on her face. "You don't know anything, Mum. Do you know that I've snogged tons of boys already? Or at least three. And I have a boyfriend, you know. Nigel is my boyfriend whether you like it or not."

As if she hadn't heard, Barbara merely said, "Where did you even *get* that skirt, dear? I don't remember buying it anywhere. It looks . . . cheap."

"Mmmm," Nichola considered, still circling the table like a hawk stalking its prey, "I suppose it *was* cheap. It was very inexpensive indeed. In fact, it cost absolutely nothing. I just put it in my bag and walked out of the store. How do you think I get all my clothes with such a puny allowance?"

Helene squirmed uncomfortably. Even she, who always spoke her mind, couldn't imagine speaking this way to her parents. And she certainly hadn't done all those things when she was Nichola's age. Or ever, for that matter. But maybe kids were more grown-up in London. Or maybe they were just more open. But she knew that if Brenda Worth had heard these words from either Helene or Alexis, both girls would have been shoved into the Audi and shipped off to therapy in less than a minute.

"Fine, have it your way," Barbara said. "Run off and have fun now. Here's some money, dear."

Nichola abruptly stopped circling. She looked distraught. Her arms snapped to cover her belly. Her shoulders slouched again. She bit a lock of hair and tried not to cry. But it was too late: Thick tears fell down her face, and she wiped them with the sleeve of her coat.

"Oh, sweetie," Barbara said, "you'll have fun today."

Nichola nodded. She was, Helene figured, strangely more upset to have won the argument than she would have been if she had lost it. "Come on then," Nichola said in the direction of the girls.

Helene and Alexis stood up eagerly. They wanted Nichola to cheer up. Permanently. For some reason both of them thought she'd stop sulking if she hung out with them. But perhaps that was just cheery optimism, because she seemed as sour as ever.

Nichola looked them up and down as she regained her composure. "We're going to Camden to see Nigel," she said with a sigh. "Look at you two. You look like such squares. I can't believe Nigel has to see me with you."

Alexis, who had gone to such lengths to change her look, was offended. "Brat," she muttered. Nichola was not the cute, adoring younger sister she'd imagined.

But Helene just laughed and said, "Think what you want, babe."

After all, there was nothing intimidating about a sulky thirteen-year-old, overdressed and awkward. Instead Helene concerned herself with Alexis's appearance. In all black, Alexis seemed unnaturally slender, like a ballerina. Then in a rare, bold move she'd added that lipstick, a shade of blood red that looked surprisingly like Helene's favorite shade. Together with Alexis's pulled-back hair and tortoiseshell headband, it was Audrey Hepburn glamour with a modern twist. Helene, who wasn't embarrassed to wear slips to school as dresses, or T-shirts sewn up as skirts, believed she never could have pulled off that style. It struck her that this is what the competition was doing to her: Instead of noticing her sister's appearance and feeling admiration and pride, all she could muster was longing and jealousy.

Well, she consoled herself, *Alexis may be the elegant one, but only I will have a ticket to the Royal Ball.* And she would soon enough, if she played her cards right. And in the meantime they were going to Camden—wherever *that* was.

10

♔

It's All Good in Camden

CAMDEN? ONE WORD: *stellar.*

Helene might have liked to see the museums, the portraits of dead kings and sketches by Leonardo da Vinci, but she could live with Camden. There were more beautiful freaks than mannequins in Madame Tussaud's: a man in a kilt and Doc Martens and a shaved head tattooed with a swirling blue and green globe; a woman with gold dreads woven with pipe cleaners so they stood straight up like Medusa's snakes; Mohawks of every color, including one painted like a rainbow, arcing over stoners' heads; girls with cat eyes; boys with their hipbones jutting out of low-slung pants posing like rock stars against the graffitied walls. Some nerds, but the cool, Emo kind: thick-rimmed glasses, sloppy hair, shirts layered over long-sleeved thermals, and Vans. Girls on roller skates, old-fashioned ones with pink wheels. And, Helene observed, you could pierce any piece of skin you wanted.

As soon as they climbed out of the Tube and began walking up Camden High Street, the main artery, Nichola tried desperately to look bored, but Helene and Alexis could tell she was as awestruck as they were. "I met him last week. He's a tweaker," she'd say of some passing club kid, or "Tim throws the most awesome parties," but the guys in question never glanced back at her. Passing before store windows, she'd yank down her minuscule skirt and cover her stomach with her coat. She'd hidden her face with her hair so that it looked like her two huge eyes were peeking out of a curtain. In other words, as Alexis whispered to Helene, she looked like a Muppet. Oddly, Alexis fit in more than she usually would, with her Goth-looking black clothes and blood-red lips. All she needed were two lines of thick black eyeliner and a rip in her fishnets.

It was a festival of freaks, and Helene had never been happier. Even the weather cooperated for once, the sun shining down, it seemed, only on Camden, only for the crazies there. A guy with a somewhat subdued pink streak in his hair approached Helene for advice on how to achieve the bright shade of fuchsia she was sporting in hers. She gave him a detailed rundown of the best procedure. His tongue was twice pierced and glittered when he spoke.

As they continued walking the streets that were lined with tattoo parlors, Helene thought maybe this was the day she should get her belly button pierced.

"No," said Alexis, pulling Helene away from the window of a tattoo parlor in which a man dressed from head to toe in black leather wielded a tattoo needle with precision. "Totally unhygienic."

Nichola bought a trucker hat, which Alexis scorned as "so last spring," but when no one was looking, she tried on one herself. It didn't go with her outfit. But a black-velvet choker with an ivory medallion of a rose did. Helene oohed over it when Alexis put it on.

What the girls were finding out was that in Camden you could buy anything you'd ever wanted. There were all the treasures Helene had scoured Urban Outfitters for, all the reasons she'd dragged Alexis to church tag sales and every Salvation Army in Westchester County. And nothing was folded neatly on shelves. Instead things spilled into the streets: racks of perfect vintage jeans, towers of granny purses, tables with the most unique handmade jewelry. Necklaces out of beer tabs; bracelets twisted from bike chains. Tents, lined up like a Moroccan village, offered flapper dresses from the twenties and tiny lace-up boots from the forties. You could buy henna hands, hair braids, your name on a grain of rice. In an hour Helene got a Celtic design painted on her forearm and a tiny fairy on her ankle. She swung a metal Strawberry Shortcake lunchbox that she'd scrounged from one of the many tents.

"I wish Laszlo and Simon could see this," she told Alexis.

"Oh, god, don't mention them. They didn't call us this morning. I thought they would. But who's waiting?" Alexis said with a wry grin. "They're not our only way to meet William. Though I sure thought they were our best."

Helene had also been wondering why the boys didn't call, but she brushed the thought aside and went over to talk to a man making tiny replicas of the *Titanic* out of toothpicks.

The phrase "vampy glamour" was going through Alexis's head as she eyed velvet corsets. Helene would look absolutely amazing in one. But Alexis was pretty sure she couldn't pull that style off; besides, she figured, she really preferred to look fancier. Her ideal shopping spree would be at Saks, not the sidewalk.

After a while Alexis left Helene cooing over sweat-stained T-shirts. She needed a break from all the people.

She slipped into a shoe store and stared at herself in its funhouse mirror. Her lips were dried and caked, and she thought they stood out too much on her face. Was she really princess material? She wasn't like Helene, who automatically smiled at everyone, giggled at every crass joke, and made boys stare at her because she was bright and sparkly like the gigantic rhinestone ring she'd just purchased and that now twinkled over two fingers.

Alexis frowned. Then she saw that when she did so, her face creased just enough to cause lines, maybe even permanent wrinkles, in her blemish-free brow. Wouldn't William prefer it if she could just relax and enjoy herself—in a vampy glamorous way? She reapplied Helene's Gash, which she'd hidden in her purse.

She smiled at her reflection. Her frown was gone, and the new application had given her lips a healthy, red glow. Of course she could pull this look off. She was Alexis Worth. She'd been photographed for British *Vogue* for goodness' sake. She *worked* for British *Vogue*. She could pull off any look she wanted—it was the thing she was best at. She began looking uninterestedly at the sneakers—when something much more important caught her eye. A newspaper lay on the counter, open to a full-page picture of Prince Charles and his sons at the Scottish shore. PRINCES OF TIDES, the paper said. William was just as poised and handsome as usual, casually dressed in a deep green sweater and khakis, but there was something in his eyes, a reserve she recognized in herself. Standing next to him was his brother—darling, cute Harry—who looked as if he had never worried in his life and who grinned at the camera like the world would always offer everything good and he'd be waiting right there to accept it. That was Helene's look. William was like Alexis, distant and aloof. After they got together, maybe she'd ask William to introduce Helene and Harry.

Unbeknownst to her, her smile crept from her mind to her lips. A skater boy who'd been watching her wasn't even on his board, and he managed to fall flat on his face.

Back in the mayhem Alexis found Helene flirting with a gypsy man who sold leather pouches. "Look," she said to Alexis, "they're for storing secret messages!" Alexis smiled. Helene was in a state of bliss, and nothing could corrupt that. Nothing, that is, except Nichola.

"Hurry up," Nichola said to Helene, who was trying on a gaggle of black rubber bracelets. "*Totally* not you," she told Alexis, who had donned a boa. "This place is so lame," she continued, fingering Alexis's boa. "It's only good if you're stoned. Then all the colors swirl together. God, do you even know what I mean? Do you even *get* stoned in America? People say it's hipper there, but I bet you haven't done half the stuff I have."

Nichola kept talking in that way as the three girls slipped in and out of tents, and up and down staircases in a rickety wooden structure, much like a boat, which was the fulcrum of the action. At what age had they started drinking? Did they like to snog boys? Because she did. At what age had they started? When did they think they would actually have sex with a boy? She'd decided to do it on her sixteenth birthday. In three years. They were sixteen, had they had sex? *As if.* Anyone looking at them could tell they were totally boring *virgins*.

It was a relief when they stopped for lunch and Nichola *had* to go around the corner to make some urgent calls on her cell. Helene and Alexis grabbed mango smoothies and tofu dogs sold by the cutest vegan hippie ever made. Or at least Helene thought so, and she told him this to his face. "It's all good," he said, grinning at her.

"It *is* all good," Helene agreed. Vegan Hippie gave them their meals at the Helene discount—for free.

The girls crammed into the corner of a picnic table. Alexis took one bite of her tofu dog and made a face—it was enough to make her long for a Central Park hot dog. Helene didn't seem to notice the gaggy, moldy taste; she finished hers in three bites, then eyed Alexis's rejected tube of reconstituted soybean paste.

"Can I have it?" she asked, and Alexis gratefully handed it over. "Do you think Nichola meant that about making out with all those guys?" Helene asked, her mouth full of tofu dog. "The only guy I'd kissed by the time I was thirteen was Billy O'Halloran. You remember, Rebecca's bat mitzvah? Oh, duh— you kissed him too!"

"Well," Alexis laughed, "we do like to share. Did you hear that Billy actually had sex with Rebecca? After the junior prom! They were both invited by juniors but ended up together at the after-party."

"Rebecca?" Helene bit her bottom lip the way she did while trying to figure something out. She was thinking of Rebecca, a smart, pretty girl who was friends with both the sisters. She'd run into her just two weeks ago at Ben and Jerry's, and they'd sat on the sidewalk and talked about their summer plans, ice cream dripping in the hot sun. She seemed the same then as she always did. "It's strange, in a way, that you can't tell by looking at someone whether they've had sex.

"I mean, it makes you a whole different person, but no one can see it." She lowered her voice and leaned over the table conspiratorially. "It's weird that there is such a gap, you know, between the other stuff and having sex." Alexis thought Helene might be hinting at something, but she wasn't sure where this was going. "There's like this vast desert between me and the girl I'll be once I'm no longer a virgin."

Helene put down her smoothie and stared at the shockingly cloudless sky. "I'll be a completely new person. Not even a girl anymore." Helene looked at Alexis, gathered her courage, and leaned into the table. "Do you think our pact is lame? To not do it until we're married?" Helene rushed out the last question very quickly and quietly.

Alexis was staring at the people walking by with plates of Indian and Thai food carrying the scents of curry and cayenne, banana and coconut. Somehow in the midst of all this activity the sisters had more privacy than if they'd been in their own room at Barbara's, and Alexis felt the urge to ask Helene what had happened between Jeremy and her. It was killing her that Helene was keeping something from her. But she was almost too proud to ask. She didn't like that she had to prod something so personal out of her best friend. *She'll tell me when she's ready,* Alexis thought.

"Hello? Lexy?"

Alexis was jerked to the present, and Helene was looking at her, expecting an answer. "I was talking to you. Were you even listening?"

"Of course I was," Alexis said.

"And?"

"And, um, I'm sure you're right," Alexis said. Helene still looked up at her expectantly.

"Do you really think so?" Helene asked in that earnest, dreamy way of hers. She seemed relieved but a bit distraught, for some reason that Alexis couldn't figure out.

Something was definitely bothering her carefree friend, and Alexis just had to find out what. This was their first heart-to-heart in she couldn't remember how long, and not once had their silly bet been mentioned.

"Helene, listen. What happened between you and Jer—"

"Alexhelene!" Nichola's anxious shout stopped Alexis midquestion. Nichola rushed up frantically, still shouting even when she was right in front of them.

"I didn't know where you were, and it's so busy and crowded in there. There was like a mob outside where this guy was beatboxing, and I just couldn't get past it, and see, we've got to go to the record store *immediately* to meet Nigel. So get up. Get up! Do you like ska? Well, do you?"

With her hands on her hips and her defiant stare, she might have looked like an underage party girl denied access to a club, but she sounded precisely like her mother.

II

You Give Punk
a Bad Name

IN THE RECORD store the walls were plastered with posters from concerts by bands none of the girls knew. The clientele was only guys, carrying those record bags that deejays—and wannabe deejays—take everywhere. All the merchandise was vinyl: ABSOLUTELY NO CDS BOUGHT OR SOLD, read a sign on the wall. Helene sidled up to a guy with blue hair and began flipping through the stacks, even though the only person she knew with a turntable was her father, and her father—well, Malibu was far away. But these albums were too good to pass up. Alexis stared at her manicure. Nichola paced the store anxiously, like a caged tiger. Every few seconds she checked her cell phone.

When the door opened, singing its two-tone chime, Helene felt the energy in the room change. She tried to keep sifting through records in the L–N bin, but someone's eyes were definitely on her. She turned around.

Surely this was not the boyfriend of Nichola Hussein?

He was a gangly punk, replete with Mohawk and pierced lip. Angry red splotches of acne dotted his forehead. Two smaller friends stood on either side of him. Nichola waved shyly from a few feet away; she'd flipped her hair in front of her face again. Nigel sneered. There was just no other word to describe it: One side of his lips curled up, the other curled down, and the result was a look of utter contempt. "Hey, Nicky," he said, "be a doll, and lend me a few quid."

When she hesitated, he turned to his friends and said in a fake working-class accent, "I can't help it if me dad's a bum and me ma's a secretary." His friends chortled like that was the funniest thing in the world. They were dressed identically to him: black Carhartts cut at the knees and black sweatshirts. Calves covered with tattoos. They all seemed to have had an unfortunate incident with a bottle of bleach. It had dyed the tips of Nigel's Mohawk orange. One friend's hair had turned surfer blond, and the other had a skunk's stripe the length of his head.

To Nichola these guys must have seemed grown-up and cutting-edge, Helene thought. But they were Helene's age, and she'd seen this type before. The kind who were materialistic and proud of every rip they made in their brand-new clothes, totally ignorant of the anarchist punk ethos. Still there was something about Nigel. When he stared at Helene, she couldn't stop staring back.

Nichola rummaged through her purse and handed Nigel five pounds. Then she stood on her tiptoes to hang her arms around his skinny chest. He shrugged them off and grabbed hold of her wrist. "I told you, Nicky, no affection in public. Not unless you're down for the deed."

Alexis gasped audibly. He was gross, and she wasn't going to stand for any more of it. Her cousin was being humiliated by a guy who was a complete loser. She wanted to be back where people were polite and made sense and wore clean Abercrombie sweatshirts and cut their hair normally. She wanted to take off the vampy Camden outfit and put on something more Upper East Side.

"Nichola," she said, glancing at her watch and feeling relieved her pale blue Cartier with diamonds was still there, "we promised to get you back by five, and it's almost six. We have to go. *Now.*"

His hand still circling Nichola's wrist, Nigel turned away from Helene to stare at Alexis. "So this must be the American cousin. Heard a bit about you. Didn't know you'd be this pretty though. And all done up like Posh Spice. I 'umbly 'ope you're 'appy wit' your stay 'ere," he said.

It was impossible to tell when Nigel was acting like himself or someone else. But Alexis had spotted the Tag Heuer on his wrist. She didn't know how much it cost in "quid," but Nigel's watch went for two thousand bucks in America. He was about as authentically punk as she was.

She was over him—and she could see from Helene's face that she was too.

"Nice to meet you, Nigel," she said in a voice that indicated it had been anything but. "And now, Nichola, we're going."

Before Helene could pick up her bags, Nigel spoke again, his voice loud and arresting like a politician's. "Hey, look, it's Pink. Is that you, Pink? Is it time to get the party started then? Pink and Posh. Two for the price of one, is it?"

Helene turned as rosy as her hair. "Yeah right," she said. And then she added, "Actually, no. Nichola," she said, smiling apologetically, "I think it's time to get back." She still wanted her cousin to like her. She even wanted Nigel to like her. Not because she liked him in the slightest, but she was used to getting along with people. Mostly because she surrounded herself with people she liked, so it was never really an issue. But the look on Alexis's face said it all: It wasn't time to get the party started. It was time to get out of there.

Nichola looked up to Nigel for approval.

"Leaving so soon, Nicky?" He dropped her wrist and gradually slid his hand down her back, coming dangerously close to off-limits territory. "Hardly got a chance to, uh, *talk* to you, if you know what I mean. Besides, I'm getting awfully tired of all this talk, talk, talk, Nicky. If I have to wait any longer for some action, I might just move on. To your cousin perhaps." He turned his sneer toward the two girls.

Helene and Alexis made instant eye contact. For the first time, they both hoped Nigel was referring to the other one.

"Nichola," Alexis said.

"You two go on without me," Nichola said in a soft, sweet voice she hadn't used all day. "Tell Mum I'll be home soon."

"No," Helene said. "We're not just leaving you here with . . . *him*." She stared at Nigel. After what he'd said to Nichola, she couldn't care less if he hated her. Besides, this was sounding way too familiar.

"And what, Miss Pink, gave you the particular impression that I treat my Nicky badly? I treat Nicky like she's made of bloody gold. Don't I? Well, don't I?"

Nichola nodded and mouthed something that Helene couldn't make out.

"Oh, come on," Helene said. "You haven't said one nice thing to her since we got here. You're just so proud of your new punk attitude. Did you buy it along with those Carhartts?"

Suddenly Nigel sneered at Helene. "Aren't you the little wannabe? All dolled up like a bad girl. Then running home to Mummy. At least your sister knows to show a little leg."

Without another word, Alexis walked out the door. Helene hesitated. "Nichola, please come with us."

"I'm *not* coming home now," Nichola said, hanging on to Nigel's arm, "so why ruin your time in London by getting Mum mad at you? You haven't seen her angry. She'll ground you, maybe even send you home. And then how will you ever get to meet stupid Prince William?"

Helene's cheeks blushed the color of Alexis's Gash lips. *That little brat has been eavesdropping on us,* Helene thought.

"*Fine.* But I don't think we'll be the ones getting grounded."

Nichola laughed. "Don't worry; I'll tell her that I refused to go with you. I'll make you look good. I promise. Cross my heart."

During the cab ride home the girls hardly talked. Normally after a day of shopping this was due to a severe case of "shopping coma," as Alexis called it: that zombielike mood you get in when you've seen too much, wanted too much, and spent too much (and in Helene's case, eaten too much tofu dog). But today there was definitely something else wrong.

"He's skeezy," Helene said. "We shouldn't have just left her there." She twisted the handle of her brown paper shopping bag between her fingers, turning them white.

"I know," Alexis said quietly. "He was so icky. Oh, and did you see his watch?"

"Yeah," Helene said. "A total poser—he's probably neighbors with Aunt Barbara and Uncle Saheed. You don't think—" She stopped herself. She didn't want to say too much about why she was so concerned for Nichola. Not yet, anyway.

"No," Alexis said. "But he's a jerk. We should try to get Nichola to see that."

"Sounds like a task for the MasterWorth Sisters," Helene said, and squeezed Alexis's hand.

They were quiet again.

It was Alexis's idea to use the servants' entrance. The last thing they wanted was a confrontation with Aunt Barbara. But Barbara, according to Basha, was out planning the orphan benefit, and the girls slunk into their room, tired from their long day. Though both of them were aware that they'd shirked their responsibility to Nichola, they were equally aware of how far apart they'd grown in the week they'd been in London. Alexis remembered her determination to ask Helene what had happened between Jeremy and her. Plan B, Helene was thinking. Plan B, Plan B!

But before either of them could say anything, they saw the note. It was placed on the table between the two beds.

girls,

A very sweet young man named Simon called. He asked if the two of you could meet him and his friend Laszlo (!) at St. James's Park on Thursday noon for a picnic and "surprise." I told him you'd be there.

Aunt Barbara

"Shall we picnic in St. James's Park then?" Alexis said, in a poor imitation of an English accent.

Helene giggled. "A very *sweet* young man," she said in Barbara's voice.

"And that exclamation point," Alexis said. "What's up with that?"

After they stopped laughing, Alexis went to the bathroom to wash the grime of Camden off her face, while Helene read Barbara's note again. And again.

Their anger had lifted; their excitement bloomed. Their concern for their cousin's welfare diminished. It would return. But in the meantime, Alexis and Helene scooped new clothes out of shopping bags. They primped and posed like models. And when Helene jumped up and down on her bed, she reached a hand out for her sister to join her.

12

The Next Best Thing
to Perfect

LASZLO GAZED AT tinned meats, while Simon pinched the produce. Neither of them had the foggiest idea how to prepare a picnic. In fact, Simon's highest culinary talent was spreading jam on toast, while Laszlo had once cooked a three-egg omelet. When they met up in the dairy section a few minutes later, Simon hefted an eggplant, and Laszlo offered a canned ham.

"I think we're on to something," Laszlo said. "Shall we slice them both and make raw eggplant-ham sandwiches?"

"No," Simon shook his head mournfully. "This is definitely not what one eats in St. James's Park on a rare sunny afternoon."

"Well, what *does* one eat?" Laszlo flung the ham in exasperation, then caught it. Simon was supposed to know about everything proper and English.

"I think we need to think of foods that go together. Think, for example, of fish and chips. Hamburgers and fries. Peanut butter and jam. Eggs and bacon. Everything has a match."

"How about, cheddar . . . ," Laszlo began, having spied an alluring slab of cheese in the fridge, ". . . and carrots? They're the same color. That means they match—at least aesthetically."

Simon looked wary until Laszlo explained himself: There were just too many food items in the store. If they narrowed down their search to, say, orange-colored foods, the shopping would go more quickly. "After all," Laszlo said, glancing at his watch, "we meet the lovely ladies in a mere seventeen minutes."

So they gathered carrots, cheese-puffs, persimmons, and Doritos with the enthusiasm boys always have when they've found a clever way around household chores. It was only while waiting in the lethargic checkout line that Simon began to worry. What if the girls weren't amused?

Laszlo waved his hand in front of his face as if brushing away Simon's concerns. "Orange is only an opening. We're British, after all. We can't woo them with food. Americans will always eat better than we do. But we *do* have history."

"So we're going to wow Helene and Alexis with our recitation of the *War of the Roses*?" Simon looked skeptical. "How about a short biography of Samuel Johnson? I hear girls love that stuff."

"Well, it became clear at Madame Tussaud's that these girls care about at least one historical figure: our fellow Etonian, William of Windsor. And why are they interested in him? Simple. It's history. He's a blood relation of Henry V and Elizabeth II. Justin Timberlake may be cute, but he lacks lineage."

Simon placed their groceries on the belt, while a disinterested checkout clerk carried on a phone conversation as she scanned them. "How exactly will their admiration of William help our cause?"

"Simple," Laszlo began. He went on to explain that the girls wanted only to glimpse William. Just like they wanted to visit the Tower of London. "It's a tourist's desire. And we'll be their tour guides. Girls *always* fall for their tour guides. It's a power thing. Girls love men in positions of power."

"Well, I did get a call about a party tomorrow night. It's at Jont's house; his folks are in Provence." Simon raised his eyebrows, inviting Laszlo to fill in the rest of the story.

"And if Jont's throwing the party, then Tim will come," Laszlo said, getting so excited he was jumping on the balls of his feet.

"And wherever Tim goes," said Simon, pocketing the change for the groceries and grabbing the bags, "Chris comes. Which means his girlfriend Tracy will obviously be there."

"And Tracy is best friends with Claudia," Laszlo continued as they walked out the door and toward the park.

"Who has been seen with our rather distant pal William all summer!" Simon concluded with a smug smile.

"Sounds like the first stop for the Laszlo and Simon Tour of the House of Windsor!" crowed Laszlo.

Alexis arrived at the park first. She looked like a runway model in a short blue dress and knee-high boots, and Simon, upon seeing her, could only say, "Oh."

"Hi," Alexis said, smiling.

"Oh," said Simon.

"Where's Helene? Am I early?"

"Oh," said Simon.

It was up to Laszlo to ask her to sit down, and to offer her some orangeade. Alexis kept smiling, but her shyness plus Simon's speechlessness made for a very awkward time.

Until Helene arrived, a half hour late. At noon Ms. Ming had asked her to call the florist—again—to check whether the roses for the Royal Ball would be the right shade of cream. "The ball's in a week, Helene; we need you every minute of every day,"

Ms. Ming had yelled when Helene finally ran out for lunch. "And you'll need to find something appropriate to wear if you plan on attending." Helene arrived, breathless from her sprint from the Tube stop and her excitement at hearing she would be attending the ball after all. When Alexis saw that Helene's cheeks were flushed the color of her hair, she asked, "What's kept you? Why do you look like you just won the lottery?"

"I'm going to the Royal Ball!" Helene exclaimed. Then, barely catching her breath, she screamed, "Orange food! That's hysterical! And it's so beautiful against the green grass. Who thought of this?"

Laszlo took a little bow.

"Genius," she said, grinning at him. "I'm going to turn this into a still life: *Cheese-puffs, carrots, and cheddar against summer lawn.*"

It turned out, however, that orange food was far better to look at than to eat. Alexis left the food largely untouched, and even Helene's aesthetic enthusiasm couldn't bring her to eat a fully orange sandwich. Fearing even a moment of dissatisfaction, Laszlo stood up, saying, "We must walk."

The four wove between the pastel blankets that dotted the grass, on each one a straw picnic basket full of proper picnic food ("How boring!" Helene whispered to Laszlo) and a scattering of toys. Toddlers chased pigeons, and nannies ran after them; the entire park looked like an unfairly matched game of tag, and sounded like an emergency: "Come back, Frederick! . . . Wait up, Cecil! . . . Cordelia, take your hands out of the goose poop! . . . Oh no, Timmy, you mustn't put that in your mouth."

On the banks of the lake elderly gentlemen rented white wooden chairs to enjoy the pale summer light, and little girls stood throwing their lunches at the ducks. The two British boys led the two American girls to a bridge that crossed the lake.

There, leaning over the railing, Simon found that he finally had something to talk about.

"That's a Steller's eider. And over there—see it, diving down? That's a goldeneye. And in the tall grasses, that's a gray heron, very fussy." He paused and Laszlo whispered in his ear, "Casually bring up William." But Simon, unsure how to do this, kept babbling.

"That colorful one's a male nene chasing the drabber lady nene in circles. Things are backward in the animal world."

Simon had been one of those overdressed toddlers who are taken daily by their nannies to St. James's Park. He'd learned to read at the tender age of three by staring at the poster of duck varieties, and he'd spent the years until kindergarten standing on this bridge naming each feathered friend below.

Alexis watched Simon carefully. She'd really never met anyone like him. He was so tongue-tied around her that he was probably smitten. But he didn't act all macho and authoritative to try to impress her. Most guys spent hours telling her how much money they would make and what kind of car they would buy and who they would draft in the NBA pick. Simon was talking about ducks! She found it surprisingly sweet and a little sexy. Alexis wondered what would have happened if she'd met him under other circumstances, sometime when she *wasn't* competing with her stepsister for the son of the heir to the crown.

Helene sat on the railing and swung her legs. They'd been across the Atlantic for such a short time, and already they'd met the most charming boys—creative and gallant and slightly mysterious. Well, she corrected herself, the second most charming boys. After William. Her mind drifted from Simon's duck monologue to her true British boyfriend. What was he doing right then? What was he looking at? *Come on, William,* she said under her breath. *Give me a sign that you're thinking of me, too.*

So you couldn't say everything was perfect for the stepsisters, but as the sun pushed its way through the nimbus clouds and light shimmered on the water below, it was the next best thing to perfect.

Laszlo, who'd caught on to the girls' good mood, was casually brushing his hand against Helene's, when the booming military march shook the air. Ducks squawked. All the birds scattered. Helene spun around to find the source of the ruckus, and there it was: Buckingham Palace in all its pinkish glory. They'd been two hundred yards away from it this whole time, and she'd had no idea!

She knew William probably wasn't there—what guy wants to visit his grandmother on a gorgeous Thursday afternoon? But he might have been there yesterday or the day before. This was clearly a sign.

"The palace!" Alexis gasped. "What's all the fuss about? Is someone walking out? Someone royal?"

"Nope, standard procedure," said Simon, sadly realizing he'd lost Alexis's attention. "Changing of the Guard."

"'They're changing guard at Buckingham Palace,'" Helene recited dreamily as she walked to the other edge of the bridge and peered at the palace. "'Christopher Robin went down with Alice . . .'"

Alexis followed Helene to the far side of the bridge. "Do you think he's there?" Her voice was brimming with excitement. "Should we go try to find him? Maybe the entire bet could be resolved today!"

Helene couldn't help but flinch a little, as she did every time Alexis mentioned her William. She told her sister that there was no way William was at the palace, because it was open for tours on Thursdays, and William hated public attention. "I read it in a guidebook," she lied.

"Well, Miss Know-it-all," Alexis said, "can you also predict the future? Can you see yourself standing at that doorway there, visiting me and my husband, William? Perhaps we'll hire you to paint our portrait."

The boys couldn't hear what the girls were talking about, but they had a strong feeling it wasn't them. So, like boys will do, they made fools of themselves to get the girls' attention.

"Don't jump, Simon!" Laszlo yelled, although Simon was standing squarely on the bridge. "Please don't leap off the bridge. It'll be okay. Your mum will love you again and forget all the questionable magazines she found under your bed. Don't end it all! You're still young!"

The girls turned away from the palace. Helene was laughing, but Alexis had a cool, practical look on her face. "Hey guys," she asked, "is it possible that you could introduce us to your friend William? We would really love to meet him."

"Well, actually—" Simon began. This was perfect! Now that Alexis had mentioned William, they merely had to demonstrate how connected they were.

"We're seeing him tomorrow," Laszlo interrupted.

"That is we *think* we're seeing him."

"Oh, come on, Simon, we're pretty sure of it. I mean, it's Jont's house. So Tim will be there. Which means that Chris will come. And his girlfriend Tracy who is best friends with—"

"We'll spare you the details, but we'd love it if you joined us."

"Of course," Alexis gushed.

Helene turned her head just a little so she could steal a glimpse of the golden Victoria Monument, in front of the palace. Then she beamed at the boys. "I wouldn't miss it."

If the palace wasn't enough of a sign, this invitation was. *I'll see you tomorrow,* she said to William. *In only a few hours.*

Glancing at her watch, Helene stopped grinning. "I have to run, or Ms. Ming will kill me."

Alexis's cool demeanor faltered. "Oh, no! I'm late for Lady Brawn's afternoon meeting."

In a flash the sisters were gone.

Laszlo watched them run away. "The plan worked perfectly!"

"I just hope he shows up," fretted Simon, as they strolled back to their food.

"Oh, no," Laszlo said, as he grabbed a fistful of Doritos. "That's not the point. See, as long as they're looking for him, we're in business. By mentioning William, we'll lead them to parties, raves . . . maybe we should invite them to the summer's end dance. But don't worry . . . by the time August rolls around, they'll have forgotten all about him. The tour guides will have prevailed!"

13

♛

The Instigators

EVEN ALEXIS HAD trouble getting dressed the next night, knowing she was going to meet William. She paced from closet to mirror, leaving eight discarded outfits in her wake. Helene was in the bathroom. She'd decided to do up her eyes like butterflies—brilliant streaks of blue and purple. Now she was regretting it a bit. There was such a fine line between looking alternative and looking like you wanted to be alternative. It was all about looking like you weren't trying. Helene was afraid she'd gone too far.

But try as they might, neither Helene nor Alexis impressed William with her entrance to the party. William didn't bat an eye at Helene's eyes or drool over Alexis's minidress, which was straight out of 1983. He didn't bring either girl a drink or light up the night with his royal smile. But William was not intentionally rude; he was absent. In fact, the party had a total population of eleven. And that was counting Helene, Alexis, Simon, and Laszlo.

One couple curled sleepily on Jont's mother's elegant couch. Another couple sat with blank looks on their faces, watching three fat carp swim clockwise in a giant tank. Two girls giggled while they munched salt-and-vinegar crisps, and Jont, the host, who was sprawled on the shag carpet, seemed too tired to get the newcomers' coats. He just waved toward the closet.

"Oh, no," Simon moaned, "there's nothing worse than a party where everyone just sits around cooly. Makes me feel so loud and hyper. I'm sorry about this. I expected more from Jont."

"Maybe we should leave and come back in an hour. It's got to pick up by then," Alexis said, trying to hide her disappointment so that Simon wouldn't feel any worse. He was so sweet to her.

"Or maybe we should just find a seat and become equally interested in the texture of crisps," Laszlo said.

As they stood in the hallway holding their coats, unsure whether to stay or leave, the front door opened behind them. A brassy, bullying voice said, "You call this a party? This scene sucks."

The guy looming in the doorway had floppy hair—not a Mohawk—and the lip piercing had mysteriously disappeared, but Helene would have recognized the voice anywhere. It was Nigel, sneering his trademark sneer, flanked on each side by his short friends. This time they had two girls with them, standing behind the boys and craning to see into the house. Neither girl was Nichola.

Alexis acted swiftly. She grabbed Helene's hand and led her to the kitchen, where they cowered behind a stove the size of a Hummer. Simon and Laszlo followed them, confused. "Is anything wrong?" Simon asked.

"What's Nigel doing here?" Alexis asked by way of reply.

"Well," Laszlo began, scrunching up his face as if the mere thought of Nigel was distasteful, "he shows up at just about every party. He's a player, you know. Got a girl pregnant last year." Laszlo blushed at this. "He is bad news. Likes to pretend he's punk and a total slummer; meanwhile, his father is Lord Something-or-other, and his mum is the Weetabix heiress. But acting punk makes him feel street. He's always trying to claim he's more street than anyone else. What a joke. He should try growing up in East London like I did."

"Wait a minute," Simon interrupted, putting a hand on Laszlo's shoulder to end his lament. "How do you girls know Nigel? You've only been here two weeks! Is there something you're not telling us?"

"He dates our cousin," said Helene, rolling her eyes. "Dates," she repeated, adding quotation marks with fingers capped by nails painted different shades of pink and purple. "We knew he was a fake the minute we saw him in Camden."

"Your cousin is Priscilla Ramsey-Boothe?" asked Simon.

"Your cousin is Genevieve Chaffen-Rawley?" asked Laszlo at exactly the same time.

It turned out that Nigel had several girlfriends, but was most often seen with Genevieve. Laszlo and Simon knew that Genevieve ran in the same circle as the best friend of the best friend of William of Windsor, but they withheld this information.

"He's grosser than I guessed," Helene said, just as Nigel walked into the kitchen and looked the girls up and down in an obvious and icky way.

"Well, if it isn't Posh and Pink. Why am I not surprised to see you little social climbers here? And with two puny Eton boys at that." He laughed for a long while. "I thought you had more sophisticated taste. I'd heard from your cousin that you were royally inclined." Another snicker. "I'll leave you *ladies* to your lemonade. I'm looking for the hard liquor. Catch you later."

As he walked away, Helene turned beet red, and Alexis became preoccupied with a bit of chipped tile. How dare he even allude to their bet! How dare Nichola tell him about it! And why did Nigel always make them feel insignificant?

Simon stared furiously at the stove, as if it had burnt him. Puny? Laszlo mulled over the phrase "royally inclined" and then put it out of his head. Nigel had always been a liar.

The silence in the room was deadly until Helene realized they all needed to be rescued. "This is ridiculous," she said firmly. "I refuse to let my evening be ruined by a snotty, spoiled poser! Laszlo, didn't you tell us Jont threw the best dance parties?"

"Well, this clearly isn't one of them," Alexis said, petulantly.

"It just needs a little help," said Helene. "We haven't even *tried*. I mean, what is this dreary music? Gregorian chant? We're not in some monastery. Hasn't anyone heard of good old rock and roll?"

Laszlo smiled. Helene could make anything fun. "Come on," he said, holding his hand out to her. "Let's go to Jont's room and raid his CDs."

Fifteen minutes later the room pulsed with rare mash-ups—Lil' Kim singing over the Ramones, the Beach Boys spliced with Tupac. While the foursome had been sulking in the kitchen, over fifty people had come to the party, and now most of them were dancing, with Laszlo and Helene in the center egging each other on. They Charlestoned. They moshed. They do-si-doed.

Alexis and Simon stayed in the kitchen for a while, talking intensely about the hassle of A levels versus SATs. When they moved into the living room and saw their friends, Alexis was struck by what an amazing couple Laszlo and Helene made.

They were both equal parts spaz and hip. *Well,* she thought, *when I end up with William, perhaps Helene will consider dating Laszlo.*

Alexis dragged Simon to the center of the room to dance with their friends. She always felt sexiest while dancing, and soon all her anxieties over Nigel faded away.

Laszlo put his arms around Helene's waist as they danced. He leaned close and whispered, "We saved the party."

Helene threw her head back and closed her eyes as the room spun around her. It was true. They were the instigators, and nothing felt better.

After over an hour of dancing, Helene, sweaty and exhausted, headed for the upstairs bathroom. But just as she walked up the stairs, Nigel came bounding down. He put an arm on either side of the banister, blocking her path.

"Hullo, Miss Pink. You're looking all hot and bothered. What have you been doing?"

"Dancing. Now will you let me get by?"

"Not so fast, baby doll. I know what girls look like after they've been doing something much naughtier than dancing. And I have to say, I think you've been up to something."

"I was dancing," Helene said, wishing she were Alexis and could glide out of this situation on her dignity alone.

"Look, luv, if you really want to win the bet against your sister . . . Aw, don't look so shocked, Nichola told me all about it. So if you're really so desperate to meet William, you should come with me to the summer's end dance in mid-August. Mr. Royal's never missed one. I suppose once you've *given yourself* to him, you wouldn't mind sharing the love with me."

She put a hand on his left arm to push it out of the way, but Nigel didn't let her. Instead, he brought his right arm around so he encircled her. She could smell him: waves of aftershave so expensive it smelled cheap, and under that just pure ick. Helene gagged.

"Or I suppose we could just do it now so you wouldn't need to waste these weeks longing for me," Nigel said softly. "I know a little room we could be alone in. Just you and me like. You're way prettier than your sister even though she's more my style. She's a little too easy, I'd say. You seem like more of a challenge. But don't worry, I'm up for it."

"Oh, Nigel," Helene whispered seductively, "that means so much, coming from you. Because you are . . ." Helene paused dramatically. Then she took a deep breath and screamed, ". . . the *grossest* guy I have *ever* seen!"

She had been prepared to spit in his face, but she didn't have to. Nigel had dropped his arms and sprinted down the stairs before she could finish her sentence.

Alexis looked horrified when Helene pulled her into the dining room and told her what had happened. "Are you okay?" she kept asking.

"I'm fine, really," Helene said. "I'm totally unscathed. I don't know about Nigel's hearing though. He did tell me about . . ." Helene was about to share her new info about the summer's end dance, when she stopped herself. Was it wrong for her to have a little information about William that was all her own? She'd tell Alexis later. ". . . Nothing. But Lexy, we've got to do something about Nichola. She cannot stay with this guy. She could get hurt!"

"I totally agree. And I know she can be a brat, but she's just young and scared."

Alexis pursed her lips as she pondered a way to help Nichola. Her answer was classic Alexis: "Shopping. Sunday. Just us girls. You have to buy a dress for the Royal Ball anyway. And believe me, you'll need my help picking it out. Working at *Vogue* has really honed my fashion sense. We can invite Nichola, but do you think she'll listen to us?"

"Of course she will. If we tell her all we learned tonight," Helene answered, but she was no longer thinking about Nichola. She was thinking about herself in a new gown, dancing with William. The Royal Ball was just one week away, and Alexis had offered to help her find a dress! She might die waiting.

Two rooms away the boys were holding their own conference in the study. They'd been planning on asking Helene and Alexis to the very formal and fancy summer's end dance, using William as their bait.

"But now I think they've started to like us just for us," Laszlo said excitedly. "This evening has been a blast, barring the brief interruption from Nigel. Maybe we shouldn't tell them about William. Let's see if they'll go with us anyway."

The boys brought more lemonade to the girls and prepared to make their offer.

Laszlo, always the clown, bent down on one knee, took Helene's hand, and said, "Fair Helene, after seeing what an insane woman you were on the dance floor tonight, I was wondering if you'd accompany me to the summer's end dance."

Helene screamed. She pulled Laszlo to his feet. Standing on her tiptoes, she kissed him smack on the mouth. When she quickly pulled away, startled at her impromptu gesture, Laszlo said with a wink, "I'll take that as a yes."

The summer flashed before Helene's eyes: She'd meet William at the Royal Ball next weekend, they'd chat, dance a little. At the dance they'd move past awkward introductions to . . . true love.

Meanwhile, Simon took a more roundabout approach with Alexis. He led her to the patio and told her in extravagant language that there was no one more lovely than she was—and no one he'd rather take to the summer's end dance. Alexis didn't have the heart to tell him that by August she was sure to have another boyfriend. And his name would be William. So mustering all her charm, she smiled and said, "Sure, I'd love to."

Simon kissed her softly on the cheek. Alexis made the smallest adjustment with her head and suddenly she was kissing Simon on the lips.

14

♚

Magda's Magic

DID THE GIRLS go to Harrods to buy Helene a gown for the Royal
Ball? No way. Did they go to Selfridges, the elite department store
that Aunt Barbara treated like her very own closet? Not a chance.
Did they visit the shops on Oxford High Street, the ones that you
drool over as you walk by? Sorry. Alexis had moved beyond the
stores mere mortals know about. Way beyond.

Very early on Sunday morning, Alexis confidently led Helene
and Nichola through the twisted streets of Neal's Yard, the hippie courtyard near Covent Garden. In a few hours the benches
would be jammed with vegans munching on tofurkey sandwiches and faux fish and chips. Soon the stores along the curvy,
cobblestone streets would be cluttered with fashionable shoppers buying Pumas in shades that wouldn't be seen in America
for another year. But now, at eight A.M., the streets were empty
and the stores closed and dark.

Except for the Neal's Yard Cheese Store. Here pleasantly
muscled men were unloading large wheels of Jarlsberg and

cheddar from trucks. With unusual confidence, Alexis walked directly in front of them and into the thickly scented air of the store. "Back door, please," she said to the bemused, overall-wearing guy behind the counter.

He grinned. "Let me escort you," he said, as he led them into a walled-in garden behind the store. Then, he turned his back on the girls, filled a brass watering can at a spigot, and began watering the many potted herbs that cluttered the yard.

At this point Helene started losing faith. She'd gone without her morning latte, as they'd arrived before even Starbucks opened, so she was especially grumpy. She knew Alexis was learning a lot about fashion and style in her internship—much more, sadly, than Helene was learning about being an artist (unless you count the fine arts of mail sorting, tea making, file labeling, and Internet searching). But Alexis, despite her beauty and persuasion, had apparently hit a dead end. It was early and chilly, and Helene wanted coffee and perhaps a pastry, not cheese. Unless maybe it was a cheese Danish.

Nichola, on the other hand, was growing more impressed as each minute passed. She knew that the hidden shop in Neal's Court was the stuff of legends. Aunt Barbara pshawed it as an urban myth and told Nichola to "stop carrying on about such nonsense." But at their exclusive public school, Nichola's classmates asserted its existence as vehemently as the Scots defend the Loch Ness monster. As the cheeseman moved from oregano to arugula, Nichola's entire demeanor changed. Her usual scowl was replaced by wide-eyed wonder, and her sarcastic tone gave way to whispered delight. In a gesture of girlish excitement, she slipped a hand in Alexis's.

Helene crossed her arms as the cheeseman placed the watering can on a wrought-iron table and wiped his wet hands on his overalls. "Hey, Lexy," she said, rather loudly, "maybe it's time for a little Plan B."

Alexis simply smiled mysteriously and put a finger in front of her mouth, shushing her sister.

"Well then," Cheeseman said, tearing off a twig of rosemary and rubbing it between two fingers, "what type of cheese will you misses be wanting today?"

"An ounce of provolone. A tad of Stilton, and . . . ," Alexis proceeded to rattle off a list of cheeses that even Nichola, who was concentrating really hard, couldn't memorize.

"A bevy of cheese then," he replied. From the pocket of his overalls he procured a set of keys. Then he walked determinedly to the wooden fence and unlocked a door that had been obscured by a fringe of ivy.

"Much obliged," Alexis said, sounding just like Lady Brawn.

The residents of Neal's Court's hidden cul-de-sac lived in near rural serenity and isolation smack in the middle of the city. Their tiny, ramshackle flats overflowed with flowers. Cars were barred; one road had been replaced by a giant communal garden, and children rode tricycles up and down the other. The complex had just one commercial establishment, which the residents allowed only because its clientele was so exclusive. Even so, the neighbors had set up the rigmarole with the cheese store to ensure the sanctity of their secret.

"Oh, my god! Oh, my god! Oh, my god!" Nichola chanted as she stood on one foot, then the other, waiting for Alexis to show them to the store. But Alexis was taking her time, savoring this moment of knowing more than Helene. And Helene was truly impressed. "So the residents wrote up that list of cheeses?" she asked. "And you actually memorized it?"

Alexis nodded regally. She knew how cool this was. "Look," she said. They were standing in front of a dark purple edifice with a minuscule sign: MAGDA'S CONSIGNMENT.

Nichola gasped. Perhaps the Loch Ness monster was real after all.

Magda sold couture worn only once. Her shop was the graveyard of Oscar-night dresses, Madonna's wedding gown (from her third wedding, the British one), Britney's concert getups, Gwynnie's ball gowns, and Sarah Jessica Parker's outfits. There was one catch: Magda sold only to a preapproved list of customers.

Alexis knocked loudly on the front door.

The door opened with a creak, and all three girls strained to look inside.

"Hullo, you are . . . ?" Magda said. She strategically blocked the doorway with her squat body, so the girls saw nothing of the dark store.

"Alexis," she said impatiently.

"Hmmm, do I know an Alexia? An Alexandra, perhaps. An Alena, maybe. I believe you are named Alejandra Magdalene, no?" Magda spoke in a foreign accent that was impossible to place. Was it French? Israeli? Moroccan? She touched Alexis's perfect jaw and moved it to the right and left as if trying to recall her profile. "I don't believe I know you, Antonia."

Nichola giggled out of nervousness.

"I was here with Lady Brawn just last week. Don't you remember?"

"Lady Brown? Now, who is this Lady Brownnose?"

It looked like Alexis had not made the list. Feeling intensely protective of her sister, Helene wanted to run away and spare Alexis the humiliation. But she fought the urge. After all, they were here so that she could find a dress to wear while she waltzed all night with William.

"Her name is Lady Brawn. She's the executive editor of British *Vogue*. One of your most loyal customers." Alexis flicked her hair. This couldn't be happening. It was like Magda had been hit on the head and lost her short-term memory!

"*Vogue. Vogue.* That sounds familiar. Is that a new type of mouthwash? Oh, I know! It is feminine hygiene product, isn't it?"

Alexis held her own. "I have a copy in my purse if you'd like to see it." She was bluffing, so thankfully Magda hooted with laughter. "Yes, yes, Alexis. You looked so delightful in the dress that my close friend Miuccia Prada made for Julia Roberts." She hooted some more. This altercation had clearly made her day, if not her week.

"I do like to see young girls flinch. It tells you so much about them. Remember, girls must be very calm under any circumstance. Except for the moment your would-be fiancé slips on the ring and during the painful hours of childbirth. Then you may scream, and a few tears would be appropriate."

"Well, that's very prefeminist of you!" Helene said under her breath. Alexis nearly threw herself on Helene to stop her from contradicting the store's proprietress.

"This is Helene," Alexis said loudly, as if she could cover up what Helene had just said. "She needs a dress for the National Gallery's Royal Ball."

"The Royal Ball. It promises to be the event of the year." At this Magda rolled her eyes back and seemed lost in thought. Finally, she turned back to Helene and stared at her. "Darling girl, for this day you must leave your feminist side at home and appear at the ball in the high heels, the made-up face, the form-fitting dress. A little submissive lady. Just like this demure one." She pointed a long red fingernail at Nichola. "If you can promise to do so, Mademoiselle Feisty, I shall find the perfect dress for you."

Magda tended to her dresses as lovingly as a gardener weeds plants or a doting old lady cares for cats. She murmured to each one, donning white gloves to rearrange a ruffle, press a pleat. "Mere finger oil can ruin fine silk," she said to the girls as she handed them each a pair of gloves to wear while browsing.

It didn't take long to find the perfect dress for Helene. Just for fun Magda had her try on the Oscar dresses of Gwyneth, Halle, and Charlize. But all along Magda knew that Helene was exactly the size of Drew Barrymore. They even had identical coloring. Lucky for Helene, Drew had been in London the previous week for a very private party. Carolina Herrera had made her a dress for the occasion. "The attendees included Miss Barrymore and four people I am not at liberty to name. But I can assure you that none of them will be at the Royal Ball. The queen will have no idea this dress was ever worn before."

Nor will her grandson, Helene thought, as she twirled in front of the mirrors. Golden satin flounced around her like the rays of the sun. The bodice was low-cut and fitted, and the entire dress was dotted with hundreds of tiny, iridescent crystals.

"Now, I hate to see any beautiful women leave here empty-handed," Magda said, scouring the racks. "Alexis, you must be needing a beaded makeup purse. It belonged to Kate Winslet, you know. Only carried it once. That's my firm policy." Magda murmured and clucked at the racks for a little while until she found what she was looking for.

"And you, little Nichola, you have such exquisite hair, dark and long and thick. You simply must have a mink stole to set it off."

Helene gasped. "Fur!"

Magda winked. "Fake mink, of course. But the finest."

Nichola squealed with delight. She threw the jet black stole over her shoulders and catwalked from one side of the store to the other.

"Beautiful, beautiful," Magda clapped. It was true. Nichola looked like an ingenue, wide-eyed yet elegant. If only Aunt Barbara could see her now.

Nichola stopped midstep and looked stricken. "But I didn't bring my purse. I haven't any money. Can I run home? I'll just be a second," she lied.

Alexis pulled out Hugo Worth's black American Express card; she'd already put her wallet in her new beaded purse. "It's on us, Nichola."

"Really?" Nichola jumped up and down.

Alexis caught Helene's eye. Helene nodded back almost imperceptibly. "There's just one thing we'd like from you," Alexis continued.

"I'll do anything. Absolutely anything." Nichola clutched her stole as if it were a baby doll.

Alexis took a deep breath before saying, "Stop seeing Nigel. He's no good for you."

In a snap Nichola changed. Gone was the almost womanly elegance and the girlish excitement. Her shoulders curved and her head bowed; her voice reached the treble of sulk; her mouth drooped into a scowl. "What are you talking about? Why would I want to do that?"

Helene grabbed her cousin's hand and held it. "Listen, Nichola, we ran into him at a party and learned some things about him. Really terrible things." She told Nichola what they knew: how Nigel dated other girls, how he got a girl pregnant. She did, however, leave out the part where Nigel trapped Helene on the stairs and propositioned her. As Helene talked, Nichola snatched her hand back and put a forefinger in each ear, saying, "I can't hear you, I can't hear you." Just like the little girl she tried so hard not to be.

Helene pleaded. "Please listen to me. You're much too good

for him, Nichola. You're sweet and beautiful, and you could get any guy. Why settle for such a loser?"

"You're just jealous." Nichola rolled her eyes in disgust. "You're making this up because you want him for yourself. Both of you do."

Helene stifled a laugh. Alexis swung her purse and said, "If he were the last guy in the world, I wouldn't go near him."

Magda, who had been in the back of the store writing up the sales slip, marched toward the girls. Everything that happened in her store was her business, so she took Nichola by the arms and looked up at the tall girl.

"My dear, dear child, if this boy is all that they say he is, why bother? I am a wise woman, and I can see some things about you. You will have many lovers in your life. A multitude. Some old. Some young. Some rich. Some poor. Your life will be filled with romance and heartbreak. Don't you worry. You miss nothing by leaving him."

Nichola's eyes filled with tears. "You just don't understand. None of you understand. He likes me. No one else likes me. No one else even bothers to notice me. He's the only person in the world to pay me any attention." With that, she flew out of Magda's store, dropping the stole on the floor.

Alexis picked up the stole as Helene rushed into the courtyard to find her cousin. But the square was empty, save for one little boy zooming around on a scooter. As she scanned the area, Helene heard the door to the cheese store swing closed. Nichola had slipped away.

"Should we run after her?" Helene asked, returning to Magda's store.

"We'll just get lost. She knows London much better than we do," Alexis said. "Besides, she's not going to listen to us now. We've only alienated her more."

Silently they paid for the dress, the purse, and even the stole. Magda delicately placed the bejeweled garments in a nondescript plastic bag. "Cheer up. Both of you. Alexis, you report to Lady Brawn that she can now send you here alone anytime. And Helene, you have a ball to attend. I foresee a very special night. A night fit for a princess."

Helene felt a shudder go down her spine and saw a look of distaste flash on Alexis's usually calm face. She clutched the bag and kissed Magda good-bye on both cheeks. Everything was about to happen.

15

♔

Cinderella's Final Hours

Two a.m., Wednesday morning. Helene Masterson kicked the duvet off her bed and stared at a water stain on the ceiling that resembled Alfred Hitchcock. She had been wide awake since the girls turned off the lights at eleven p.m., and it began to seem like she would never sleep. This had been happening all week. During the days, Ms. Ming worked her relentlessly in preparation for the benefit. During the nights, Helene's mind raced with the potential events of the weekend. She'd never been so excited in all her life. Perhaps that was because she'd never wanted something so badly before. This wasn't like begging for a swimming party or a mountain bike. Those were childish desires. William was a new want, a grown-up want. And it kept her up.

As a car drove down Whittington Place, a shaft of light rode across the girls' bedroom. All at once the golden dress, which hung from the closet door, was illuminated; its gems glowed like a lit chandelier. Drew's dress. Now it was her dress, and it was so beautiful that Helene didn't want to close her eyes. She wanted to stare at it all night. Finally, at two forty-five, exhaustion got the better of her, and she was dragged into sleep.

Three A.M., Wednesday morning. Alexis's eyes snapped open. She'd been dreaming something awful, but she could recall only one image: There was a *Vogue* photo shoot at the Worths' house in Scarsdale. Alexis animatedly told Lady Brawn that she *lived* there, and she should definitely be in the shoot. Lady Brawn shot her a piercing look. "You're just our coffee girl, Alexis. We already have our model." And there, walking down the Worths' staircase, was Helene. She'd become a mermaid. Her head was the same, but her dress—Drew's dress—was a fish's tail. A thousand photographers snapped her photo, and her jeweled scales reflected the glow of each flash.

It was only a dream, she told herself. Only a product of the imagination. Just in her head. But like all dreams, it held a tremor of truth that made it impossible for Alexis to return to sleep: She had never worn something so finely made, so simultaneously au courant *and* timeless. And she was the stylish, beautiful sister! Alexis could already see the society pages of *Hello!*: *American girl in a one-of-a-kind Caroline Herrera dress waltzes seamlessly into British society after William asks her to dance. . . .* Alexis stopped herself. Jealousy was wasted energy. It only prevented you from achieving your goals. It was like racing a horse on a lame leg—you couldn't win. The best thing to do with jealousy was to push it away. But Alexis had been doing this all day long, and at three forty-two she was watching the digital clock's display, trying to stop time, trying to make the weekend never come.

That evening Alexis made plans to eat sushi with Lucille, Isabelle, Tabitha, and Caro, the other interns from British

Vogue. But as soon as the lacquered tray of raw fish arrived, she began picturing Helene the way she looked in the dream: as a stunning mermaid. Alexis lost her appetite for hamachi and fatty tuna.

"I think I'm coming down with something. I need to go home," she said. The four girls held their chopsticks in the air and looked at Alexis incredulously.

"So this is how you stay so thin! I thought so," said Tabitha meanly. For the last month she'd been jealous that Lady Brawn gave Alexis the most responsibility.

"It's true," said Caro, who had been bumped from working on photo shoots when Alexis arrived. "I've never even seen you eat during lunch breaks."

"No, it's not that at all; it's just that my sister . . . ," Alexis stopped. Why explain her petty jealousy to Tabitha or anyone else? She was Alexis Worth! She picked up her purse and rushed out of the restaurant, saying, "I had a great time. Maybe next week."

For once Alexis chose to walk home instead of taking a cab. She craved the anonymity of the city streets and wanted to curtail the time spent at home with a gushing Helene. It was drizzling slightly, and in her rush she'd left her umbrella at the restaurant. But she didn't care. The rain seemed to suit her mood—if not her suede boots.

Why had she agreed to this bet? It used to be that Helene and Alexis would do totally different things on a Friday night, and Alexis never worried. Alexis would be at a movie with one group of friends, and Helene would be at a party with another, and jealousy never crossed their minds.

A group of guys passed, almost stumbling over their own feet when they saw her, so dark and brooding in the rain. One of them looked like Simon—same hair, same shy grin—and she almost ran after him. That was silly. Why would she think of Simon at a time like this?

The next day at work, Tabitha started a rumor that Alexis had an eating disorder. Caro swore that she'd never seen Alexis eat more than an apple. And only half of that.

"She's a classic anorexic," Caro whispered to every *Vogue* staffer she saw.

Alexis felt she couldn't eat her customary yogurt and sandwich in the staff dining room because everyone would be watching. She stormed out of the office with her head high. Why did people always want to cut her down? Girls believed that everything was so easy for Alexis, so effortlessly flawless. They had no clue how much work—how much anxious planning—went into her calm exterior. She studied, worked, and dieted like the rest of them. Maybe she just tried harder.

Her hands were shaking as she spooned her yogurt while standing under a dripping awning down the street from *Vogue*. She knew she could return to the office and tell them the truth. Yes, she dieted. She'd been dieting since those awful weeks when she was eight and her mother fed her only grapefruit and cottage cheese. But she'd never starved herself. So why *didn't* she confront the rumors? Alexis had no idea.

She began to unwrap her peanut butter and jelly sandwich. Maybe she didn't want to tell the truth because she liked the attention—even if it was negative attention. What a terrible idea! Alexis set half her sandwich on a window ledge and leaned against the glass, contemplating. Could she stoop so low?

But why not? Helene was getting all the attention at home. Every evening Aunt Barbara begged for more details of the Royal Ball. Are there lilies in the floral arrangements? Will you decorate the crudités with kale leaves? Who RSVP'd? And tomorrow William himself would be fawning all over Helene.

Luckily Alexis's phone rang before she could sink into the whirlpool of jealousy that consumed her at night. "Hey, Simon. What's up?"

"Alexis, hi! I was just wondering if you wanted to come to a rave with me this Friday. It should be cool."

Alexis looked out at the passing traffic. Friday night was the Royal Ball. She'd be so preoccupied by Helene's adventure that she'd be in no mood to party. Besides, since William would be attending the ball, there was no chance he would be at the rave.

"Sorry, Simon. I have some, um . . . some things to do that night. Some other time, okay?"

When Alexis returned to *Vogue,* Caro told her with a smug smile that Lady Brawn wanted to see her. "Immediately. She sounded rather huffy."

Alexis entered the editor's lavish office. Lady Brawn watched her silently. She didn't speak as Alexis sat in her customary chair, and she didn't answer when Alexis asked how she could be helpful.

Finally, taking a deep drag on her cigarette, Lady Brawn spoke. Alexis expected to be reprimanded for an imaginary eating disorder, but instead she heard Lady Brawn speaking about Prince William. *William!*

"You see, my dear girl, *Vogue* hasn't done a photo spread of our nation's most eligible bachelor since before the dark days of his mother's death. We tried to keep our distance, didn't want to stoop to the tactics of the hungry paparazzi. But now William is a pinup. He is an icon. He is a monarch-in-training. And he is a sweet, sweet boy. I want *Vogue* to show the world these many sides of William. What do you think?"

Stunned, Alexis could only nod.

"I spoke with his people this morning, and they are *very*

interested. *Very* interested. He's been so misrepresented by the press, you know."

Alexis shook her head in sympathy with William's plight.

"Now, I hope you're not too busy for the next few weeks, because we've scheduled the shoot for three weeks from this Friday. And I want you to be the point person. William will need to know where his clothes are kept. He'll need to be fed. And you'll be in charge of all these details. Is that understood?"

By now Alexis had abandoned her calm facade. "Oh, yes, Lady Brawn," she squealed. "I can't wait!"

Even Lady Brawn allowed a hint of a smile on her otherwise implacable face. "Perhaps you'll spend this evening doing a little Internet research on his coloring. We'll need to pick at least six or seven outfits for him. Or do you have other plans?"

"Nothing I can't cancel," Alexis said.

16

Thank God It's Friday Night

"TWO PEACOCKS SOAKED in rum."

Laszlo felt extraordinarily small next to the truck-sized bouncer who barred entrance to a warehouse in East London. He hadn't thought much about the password that had shown up in his e-mail, but it sounded pretty silly now that he was saying it out loud to a man who seemed wider than he was tall.

"All right. You're in," the bouncer said, moving aside.

Inside, the rave was well under way. Laszlo spied a group of girls he and Simon had hung out with the previous summer.

"Should we go say hello?"

Simon shrugged. "Maybe in a bit."

Laszlo understood. He'd totally lost his interest in flirting since he'd met Helene. This was strange. Even when he was dating Katrina, he loved talking to other girls. He'd never cheated—but he enjoyed the game of it. Now he wasn't even going out with Helene, but he didn't want to meet anyone else. "We'll talk to them after we have a drink."

"Or two," Simon said, handing Laszlo a plastic cup of Red Bull and heading to an old tattered couch in an empty corner of the room where they could sit amid the thunk-thunk of the beat and not talk to anyone.

"I'm sorry, I didn't catch that. Helen is your name? Well, Helen, you look simply ethereal, waifish, celestial . . ."

The man in front of her was a self-proclaimed famous poet. That's how he introduced himself: "Let me make your acquaintance. I'm T. P. Bradford. Yes, I admit, I'm the famous poet." Helene had only said her name and he'd begun his monologue. The Famous Poet was skinny and giraffelike: His neck was preternaturally flexible. Helene tried unsuccessfully to peek around him to see if William had made his entrance. But every time she adjusted her head, she was staring again at the pimples on the Famous Poet's neck.

"That dress is gossamer, and your form is serpentine, statuesque. The way you look amongst the artwork is resplendent, effulgent. . . . Oh, silly me, you are but a child. Do you even know these words? Shall I teach them to you?"

Helene, whom Alexis called "The Walking Dictionary," saw her escape. "Actually, sir, I have no idea what you are talking about. Now if you'll excuse me, I think Ms. Ming is calling for me."

Helene had been avoiding Ms. Ming's beseeching gestures all evening, but now she felt compelled to search out her boss at the drinks table. The gallery did look stunning. Ethereal, in fact. Even resplendent. But Helene didn't like how the art was ignored. These pieces—by Monet, Velasquez, da Vinci, van Gogh—were never intended to be backdrops to a social scene. They spoke of love and torment, the end of the pastoral life, and the beginning of modernism. Tonight, however, they were just accessories to all the beautiful women.

Like herself. Something had changed when Helene put on Drew's dress. Helene was beginning to realize that this was how her sister must feel every day. With each step Helene took through the gallery, men's eyes flashed toward her, like a school of fish all turning together. Even if a man was speaking to a woman, a graceful woman in a slinky dress, Helene noticed, his eyes adjusted ever so slightly to take in the sight of Helene crossing the tile floor.

"Quick," Laszlo said, "look deeply involved in conversation."

"About what?"

"Anything at all. Nigel and Chaffen-Rawley are headed our way, and I can't bear hearing his voice tonight."

No such luck. "Scoot over," Nigel said, as he pushed his way between the two friends and sank onto the couch. "Bugger off for a few minutes, Genevieve," he said. "Be a good girl and bring me a drink."

"Is there anything you were wanting, Nigel?" Laszlo asked. "Because we're having a rather urgent conversation."

"Oh, really?" Nigel cackled. "Were you relaying fantasies about loose American girls?"

"Please," Simon said, "it's really none of your business."

"Well, a certain girl I hang out with from time to time happens to be the cousin of your American friends. And she happened to ask me yesterday if I had another girlfriend. One by the name of Genevieve. Now where do you think she got that information?"

When no one replied, Nigel answered himself: "Perhaps she heard it from her American cousins? And perhaps they heard it from you, their escorts?"

"Well, it's true, Nigel," Laszlo said. He was scrunched up against one arm of the couch. "You *are* going out with Genevieve. It's not like a secret or anything."

"I denied it, of course. I like to keep my girls separate. And I'd appreciate you not messing with my system." Nigel spread his legs and leaned back into the couch, making himself more comfortable. "By the way, isn't it a bit sad the way you're chasing after Helen and Lexy or whatever they're called, what with the bet and all."

"What bet?" Simon asked, practically falling off the cushion to make room for Nigel's legs.

"Come on, don't tell me you didn't know." He looked right and left to see their reactions.

"We have no idea what you're talking about," Laszlo said, despising himself for speaking with Nigel at all.

Nigel beamed. Apparently, nothing made him happier than relaying awful information. "Don't you get it? Your little girl-friends aren't interested in you. They're just using you to get to Prince William. They've made a bet."

Simon looked at Nigel suspiciously.

"What kind of bet?"

Nigel sneered. "What kind do you think?" He laughed then. "Whatever. I'll catch you two losers on the flip side."

Before Helene reached Ms. Ming (who had drunk too many cocktails to care where her intern was), she was intercepted by a short man with a crooked toupee. "You must be Dame Carlton's youngest. All grown-up now! Don't you remember me? Peter Roberts? I dandled you on my knee when you were just a little girl."

"Sorry, I think you're mistaken. My name is Helene."

The man scratched his head, causing his toupee to fall toward his left eye. "Ah, yes. Helene Van Wyck. I haven't seen you since you wore pinafores. I was a great favorite of your late father's."

Luckily this man was so short that Helene could peer over him to watch the door. But William didn't enter. "Listen, sir. I don't think I'm anyone you know. I'm not a Van Wyck or Carlton or anyone like that. I'm an American."

"Nonsense, child. I've never seen a more typical British beauty. An English rose. A perfect English rose. Peaches and cream. Stop putting on that American accent this minute and stand up for your country and your queen."

"But it's not an accent. This is how I speak."

The man nearly shook with rage. "Oh, you British girls all want to be American these days. You have no sense of pride in our great nation. I cannot bear to talk to you any longer." With that, he huffed away.

Alone in the center of the room, Helene realized with a shock that she was totally bored. The other interns were all giggling together in a corner, hoping some guy would come and ask them to dance. She looked around the gallery. Here were the richest people in all of London, and they looked silly, like mannequins in a store window, like dogs at a dog show. The women wore bows where nothing needed tying. They wore more layered ruffles than a wedding cake, and hats that resembled pincushions. Cleavage fell out when it shouldn't. Dark foundation failed to cover up the pasty skin of a sunless city. She wished she had someone to make fun of it with. Laszlo would have a field day. He'd be imitating the penguin walk and dress of the men in tuxedos. He'd put on an accent to break the decorum of the dour women. He'd ask Helene to dance and waltz her around, Fred Astaire to her Ginger Rogers. He'd stand silently, breathlessly, in front of the Rembrandt with her, forgetting there was a party.

Helene didn't feel like herself. She wanted to wash the goopy makeup off her face and exchange the gold strappy heels for her red cowboy boots. *I see why you wore this dress only once,* she told Drew. *It's gorgeous. But it's not me.*

Classic summer complexion, Alexis wrote in a notebook. *Would look good in all shades of blue. Stay away from oranges and browns. Green could work. The color of fertilized grass in Westchester. No earth tones—those are for commoners. Purple is regal but perhaps a little too much for his skin. Could try pink!*

There was a commotion by the door. The violinists interrupted whatever concerto they were playing and struck up "God Save the Queen." Guests from all parts of the gallery headed to the entryway. *William?* Helene asked. *Is that you?*

She ran in a most unladylike fashion toward the forming crowd and found herself next to Ms. Ming. A few Royal Guards entered, looking like Russians in their black fur hats. Next came the more traditional security guards, hefty men in black suits wearing an earpiece in one ear. Finally . . .

"Is that Prince Edward?" Helene asked Ms. Ming, unable to contain her disappointment. The doors had closed; the entire entourage had entered.

"Yes," Ms. Ming gushed. "Edward. Isn't he handsome!"

"Isn't anyone else coming? Like William or Harry or Charles or someone?"

Ms. Ming shook her head without looking at Helene. She was unable to keep her eyes off Edward. "Of course not. Edward is our royal patron this year. I thought I told you. I couldn't be more pleased. He is, you know, the queen's youngest son." Ms. Ming tugged up her slipping-down strapless dress, and furiously batted her eyelashes as Edward approached, stiff as an undertaker in his dark suit.

"And the baldest," Helene whispered, just as Edward reached over to shake Ms. Ming's hand.

"So pleased to meet you, Your Royal Highness," she cooed, extending her hand. "This is *such* an honor."

But Edward wasn't angling for Ms. Ming's hand at all. He locked eyes with Helene and grabbed her hand in both of his.

"And then," Helene told Alexis later that night, her dress thankfully hung back on the closet door, "Edward told me he was *delighted* to meet me. And he's William's *uncle*! So, Ms. Lexy. I hate to say it, but *technically* I'm winning the bet."

"Congratulations!" Alexis gushed. This was without sarcasm. She was truly happy that her sister had had a little fun. Tomorrow Helene would learn what she was up against.

17

♔

Can You Have Your Cake and Eat It Too?

AT NOON THE next day a very tired Simon and Laszlo argued as they ate cold pizza in Laszlo's kitchen. The rave had gone on until the wee hours of the morning. "He's a liar," Simon said. "You know that. Nigel's blagged since the day he walked into Saint George's Primary School and told us he was Superman's son."

But Laszlo wasn't so certain. The girls did seem a little too excited every time they heard about William. "If this is true, I'm going to tell Helene I can't hang out with her," Laszlo said. "I may be only one one-hundred-twelfth royal, but I have a little pride."

Simon nodded and the two boys sat there, pondering a summer without Alexis and Helene. Even though they'd known the girls for only two weeks, this seemed impossibly bleak and awful.

"The thing is," Simon finally said, "I just like hanging around them so much. I wouldn't mind still playing the role of London

tour guide just for that pleasure. Even with their stupid obsession with William."

"You know, we're never going to get anywhere with them,"
Laszlo said, sounding like a man sentenced to prison.

"I thought you actually liked Helene," Simon spat back. "As a
person."

"Yeah, as a gorgeous, adorable person who is totally not into
me."

"Well, you can't have her," Simon said sullenly. "So the question becomes, Do you still want to hang out with her?"

"Every single day," Laszlo sighed.

Simon jumped up so quickly that his chair fell over. "Listen!"
he demanded, although Laszlo was already listening. "We can't
give up. We've barely tried to win these girls. Let's forget the
bet. Nigel's probably making too big a deal out of it. We'll
show the girls London. . . . We'll get to know them. . . . They'll
start to forget the bet. And then, we'll do something really big.
Some grand gesture that will show them how much we like
them."

Laszlo raised his eyebrows. "What will this grand gesture be?"

Simon shrugged. He had no idea, but it sounded romantic.
"Only time will tell."

Laszlo thought about it. Maybe with someone as interesting
as Helene, you just took what you were offered. Maybe. But
maybe not. Only time would tell.

Laszlo stood up and reluctantly raised his slice of pepperoni.
"To the grand gesture!" he said.

Simon and Laszlo took the girls out every weekend. They sat
with them in the swinging capsules of the London Eye, a giant
Ferris wheel that offered sweeping views of the city. They drove
the girls to Cambridge and punted down the river. They showed

off the street markets of East London and had dinner in the curry houses of Brick Lane.

Helene and Alexis enjoyed themselves, but their minds—and hearts—were otherwise engaged. After the party at Jont's, they'd vowed never to kiss the boys again—it went against the spirit of the bet. Now they were both waiting to see what would happen when Alexis turned her blue eyes on William and led him to his changing room.

The weeks of waiting were especially excruciating for Helene. Every evening Alexis would come home with a new detail: what type of undershirt William liked to wear, how she had ordered German ham because it was his favorite. Helene just knew that as soon as William saw her sister, the bet—and Helene's whole life—would be over.

The day before the photo shoot, Alexis was on top of the world. She felt so warmly about everyone at *Vogue* that she decided it was time to dispel the nasty rumor circulating about her. On the way to work she stopped at a bakery and bought the most decadent chocolate cake available. Layers of hazelnut butter frosting, interspersed with slabs of rich flourless chocolate cake, topped by a cloud of whipped cream.

That afternoon Lady Brawn—who'd been eager to go along with Alexis's plan—spoke menacingly into the intercom. "Tabitha, Isabelle, Lucille, and Caro! Your presence is requested in my office. Immediately."

When the girls nervously entered, Lady Brawn attempted a smile. "Now, you may have forgotten, but today is my half birthday. And as I celebrate my full birthday with my senior staff members, I always like to have a smaller celebration on my half with the interns. Oh, don't worry about gifts; a card will do. Alexis was kind enough to bake us her favorite dessert."

Alexis cut everyone a sliver of cake, and then treated herself to a large wedge. Of course, the thought of all that butter and egg made her gag, but she didn't let on. She closed her eyes dreamily and bit down, with visions of William dancing in her head.

At nine that evening Alexis was still at work, the only one left in the *Vogue* offices. She'd checked in with the caterers and the photographer. She'd talked some sense into the impetuous hairdresser who wanted to dye Will's golden trusses black. She'd located the socks for the bedroom scene, ironed the seersucker shorts for the camel-riding outfit, and found a replacement for the wool evening coat that had been horribly mishandled by the tailor. She'd updated Lady Brawn's BlackBerry down to the minute—and left a printout on her desk. In fact, every item on Alexis's neatly handwritten list was meticulously crossed off. But something was not quite right.

And that something was Alexis's shins. They itched.

Okay. So that's not the end of the world, right? The perfectly-put-together girl has some itchy shins. Big deal.

But this was no normal itch. Her shins itched like poison ivy. Or worse. They itched like an attack of fire ants. She looked down and saw that both shins were swollen and red. Without pausing, she wrote on her list: *Wear boots tomorrow.* Then she carried a vase of poppies from the reception area to her desk, just in case William happened to see her workspace. She wanted it nicely decorated.

But suddenly she had to get rid of the vase, nearly dropping it on the floor, because her arms had lit on fire. They were hotter than sunburn. Large welts crisscrossed the length of her forearms. And they itched like crazy.

Five minutes later it was her thighs. Then the skin on her belly. Then her lower back. Alexis sat on the floor of the bathroom, pressing wet paper towels to her skin. It would all be fine, she told herself. She'd wear tights. Long sleeves. Gloves, if necessary.

But then she glanced at her reflection in the mirror. Her left eye was so swollen it looked bee-stung. Her jaw and cheeks were just beginning to turn crimson.

Alexis called a cab.

Later that evening, when Alexis was lying in bed, unable to bear even the lightest sheet as a cover, Aunt Barbara came in with the doctor.

"I feel so stupid, Aunt Barbara. I usually check to see if there are hazelnuts in things, but this so clearly said, "chocolate cake.""

Alexis thought of her blunder and tears ran down her face, but she lacked the energy to brush them away.

"Oh, sweetie, don't worry. Doctor Peterman will take care of you and get you a prescription for allergy medication. Saheed will go to the pharmacy on his way home. And the doctor promises that you'll start feeling better in twenty-four hours."

Twenty-four hours! Alexis didn't say anything until Barbara and the doctor left. But when she was alone in the room, she began to cry even harder. She threw a box of tissues against the wall and stomped her feet and swiped a stack of magazines onto the floor. "It's not fair," she wailed. "It's not fair. It's not fair. It's not fair."

Helene found no relief in Alexis's missed chance. And when Lady Brawn called the next evening to tell Alexis how wonderfully the shoot had gone, thanks to all her preparation and foresight, Helene shared her sister's grief. But when Alexis's hives disappeared, and her father sent her the most scrumptious bouquet of pink roses, Helene allowed herself to consider Prince William. Now she had a chance again. But she had to hurry up. It was late July. The summer—and the bet—were halfway over.

18

♛

Emergency Procedures

THE DAYS THAT passed after the missed photo shoot were the glummest since Hugo Worth found Alexis and Helene fighting like caged tigers over a bead necklace and didn't let either of them attend a party at Six Flags Great Adventure. That is, these were the glummest days since back before Plan B. There'd been no clues to William's whereabouts; the sun had been hiding for ten days; Simon and Laszlo, growing tired of the girls' bad attitudes, stopped calling so often; and Nichola—after screaming, "He promised he's not dating anyone named Genevieve. You're the liars!"—had stopped speaking to them entirely.

One dreary Saturday found the sisters sitting on a park bench in Russell Square, unenthusiastically debating where they should spend the day.

Helene, as usual, opted for the wonders of the British Museum. And Alexis, as always, pointed out that artifacts hosted dust mites, and there was a midsummer sale at Theory, just down the block on Covent Garden. But neither sister cared very much where they went.

They watched the au pairs and the divorced dads chase after each other's kids. They watched the fountain rise and fall. They watched a homeless man wake up and then start snoring again. They watched a gaggle of skateboarders cut through the park, followed by four teenagers, two girls and two boys, giddy with each other. They were French. You could tell because the boys carried fluorescent backpacks and the girls wore strange scraps of sweaters and still looked ravishing.

Of course, these couples had to sit on a bench directly across from Helene and Alexis. Of course, the girls had to giggle like the boys had said the funniest thing in the world. And of course, each couple had to start making out passionately.

"I gotta get out of here," Helene said. "I can't watch this."

"I know. It's killing me. But where should we go? I'm embarrassed to say this, but I don't really feel like shopping."

"And I couldn't really care less about art right now. God, we're so pathetic. We don't want anything."

"Well, I do want a Diet Coke. That's something."

The girls fulfilled their meager desires at a newsstand down the street. Alexis was paying when Helene shrieked, "Oh, my god! Oh, my god!"

"What?" Alexis whipped around.

"Look!" Helene swept her hand over the spread of tabloid newspapers that covered three shelves of the newsstand.

> WILLIAM AT RACY YACHT RACES
> FREE WILLIE
> WILLS PLAYS YACHT-SY
> YACHTS FOR A FUTURE KING
> WILL WILLIAM SKINNY-DIP?
> MALTA MAKES WILLIE HAPPY

"Who's Malta?" Alexis asked bitterly.

"Silly. Malta's an island. William must be vacationing there."

"They'll do anything to run a picture of him shirtless," Alexis said, shaking her head like a seasoned member of the media.

The girls bought all six tabloids and brought them back to the park to read. Thankfully, the making-out Frenchies had gone away, and Helene and Alexis could squeal undisturbed. The wind had picked up, and Alexis held the pages down while Helene read out loud; it turned out that you had to cooperate to compete.

Tabloids are not known for their probing journalism, and the papers were short on facts. They gave only the vaguest details of William's itinerary, and none of them answered the most important question: Was he on the beach with a girl? But the articles did agree on one thing. William was "sure to turn up" at the yacht races off Malta in mid-August.

"Malta," Helene said wistfully, "in the blue Mediterranean. It's the land of Homer, Alexis. Of course he's going there!" Helene had a love for Homer that went beyond her encyclopedic knowledge of all things literary: She felt a strong bond with Helen of Troy.

Alexis wasn't jealous of Helene's know-it-all-ness. This is where the sisters differed. Helene *should* know all about the *Odyssey,* just as Alexis should know exactly what to wear when they got off the plane in Malta. Because they had to go.

"We totally have to," Alexis said. "There's no way around it. I don't want to hear any excuses."

"But—"

"Nope," Alexis interrupted. "I'm sick of moping. Remember, this is summer *vacation.* We're supposed to have fun. We're Helenalexis. We can go to Malta. We can go anywhere."

"It's just that—" Helene looked unpersuaded.

"Not a chance." Alexis was folding up the papers.

"But, Alexis," Helene spit out, "how can we go to Malta? I actually have no idea where it is."

At that, Alexis burst out laughing. "Well, *I* thought Malta was a person. Okay, all we need to do is find out where Malta is. Then we're buying plane tickets for the weekend of the yacht races."

"If it's reasonable. Should we look in a book?" Helene asked. "The British Library is a few blocks away."

Alexis yawned. "I'm much too excited for some dumb library. I know how we'll find out. And she proceeded to text both Laszlo and Simon: *Impt. question. Russll Sq. ASAP.*

"Malta?" Simon asked incredulously. "That was your urgent question?"

Alexis smiled her most winning smile. "We're naturally curious about geography."

"Well, be curious no longer, fair ladies," Laszlo said, doing his best impression of a sexy tour guide. "Sitting in the middle of the Mediterranean, Malta may be small, but its historical significance is significant indeed. The Knights of Malta saved Europe from the Ottoman Empire, and then in the Second World War—"

"He did a report on Malta in fifth form," Simon whispered conspiratorially. "He even, if I remember correctly, tried to join the Knights of Malta himself."

"Well, you did ask," Laszlo complained. "I was only trying to help."

"We just want to know things like, Can you fly there? Do they speak English? How do you get on a yacht?" Alexis explained.

Simon noticed the newspapers that covered the bench like a blanket. A headline caught his eye: WILL'S SUMMER VACATION IN MALTA. "Aha!" he yelled. This was no mere history lesson. "So that explains the sudden interest."

"He must have chosen Malta because of its history," Helene said eagerly. "I mean, he must want to go somewhere that was in the *Odyssey!*"

Laszlo eagerly explained why William would go to Malta. "This race you're talking about—the Smarties Grecian Mediterranean Cup—is usually, well, in Greece, of course. But when William said he'd like to be the extra man on the *Blueblood* crew, they had to move the entire race to accommodate the crowds. And I hate to tell you this, but William may be the first heartthrob to sail there: Odysseus bypassed Malta entirely."

"Actually," Helene piped up, "you're totally wrong. It is believed that Odysseus spent seven years in Malta. That's where he was imprisoned by Calypso in her cave. You know, she promised him immortality if he'd stay with her."

"Right!" Laszlo smiled. "Calypso's cave. That's where Odysseus was a prisoner of *love.*" He widened his eyes when he said this.

Helene blushed, trying to think of a witty retort. Luckily, Alexis grabbed her arm and shrieked, "He's participating! We're going to see William sail a boat!"

Laszlo caught Simon's eye and frowned. So this was how it would always be with the girls. He would chase Helene, who would chase William. He shook his head. That kind of subservience was not for him. "Simon, don't we have to get back to our video games?" he asked.

"You're going to . . . ?" Simon asked, ignoring Laszlo. Desperation made his voice crack. "To Malta?"

Alexis looked at Helene curiously. "Aren't we?"

Helene saw William, her William, steering a boat to safety while the waves crashed on the sides. (She imagined it was a dangerous voyage, not a mere yacht race.) She saw him gallantly calming a scared child and maneuvering a careening craft away from a breaching whale. With this image in her head, she reached into her messenger bag and pulled out Hugo Worth's American Express card. "If anything qualifies as an emergency," she said with a grin . . . *How much can a trip to Malta possibly cost?* she thought with a twinge of worried guilt.

19

The Grand Gesture

ON THE FRIDAY night before the yacht race, Helene and Alexis sat at the dinner table. Helene asked Aunt Barbara to pass the peas, and then she mentioned with a totally straight face that she and Alexis were going to the Glastonbury Festival all weekend. Nichola, who had been ignoring them for weeks, finally showed some interest.

"Oh, lucky you. All the best bands are going to be there. Mummy, can I—," but she stopped herself, remembering that she was no longer friends with her cousins.

Distracted as usual, Aunt Barbara merely smiled at the girls. "You have a nice time now. And dress warmly. I hear it gets terribly damp and chilled in that part of the country."

"Definitely," Alexis said, although at that moment she had a suitcase filled with new bikinis, halter tops, and sundresses. Average August temperature in Malta? Ninety degrees.

Perfect for tanning. Perfect for swimming. Perfect for meeting a prince.

Only one thing was not perfect: their strategy for finding William. In fact, after taking a cab to Heathrow and boarding Air Malta flight two at seven in the morning, Helene and Alexis's plan was extremely foggy. They had no idea where they were going to stay. They didn't even know the names of the towns.

Alexis wasn't concerned. "It's an island," she told Helene as they got in the cab. "How large can it be?"

But as the airplane rushed east and Alexis slept peacefully, Helene clutched her coffee. Alexis believed that because they were rich and cute, everything would work out for them. Well, someday that would stop being true. What if that day was today?

"Newspaper, miss?" the flight attendant asked, refilling Helene's coffee.

Helene clutched the paper as if it would give her some answers. And it did. There was William on the front cover. He was in a café. And he was also drinking coffee! *William enjoys the view in the Maltese town of Valletta before the big race,* read the caption.

Hi, Helene whispered.

Hey, Helene. I knew you would come visit me here. After all, you're Helene of Troy. Launcher of a thousand ships. Well, at least launcher of my yacht. Tomorrow morning, that is. I can't wait to see you, William whispered back, and Helene's anxieties sailed away into the blue Mediterranean waters.

Alexis did believe that good things would happen to her. But this wasn't simply because she was rich and drop-dead gorgeous. After all, her looks and money had done nothing to soothe the pain when her mother up and left her. Alexis believed that the future would turn out wonderfully because she did absolutely everything right. She wore the right clothes; she dated the right boys; she did well enough at school; she definitely had the right internship this summer. Because of this, she'd go to the best college, meet the most gorgeous husband, land the coolest job in the fashion industry. It was an equation: If you did the right thing, then good things happened.

And so while Helene downed her third cup of coffee, Alexis woke up and stretched her arms, contented as a kitten. After all, meeting the future king of England while she was wearing a Juicy bikini would clearly be the right thing to do. When the plane landed, she marched off to claim her two Louis Vuitton suitcases (yes, all for one weekend) and find her way to the prince. It was Helene who dawdled, taking in the adorably small airport, the immediate smell of sea air, and the concern that there was no map of the island available at the gift shop—because there was no gift shop. When Helene (who hadn't needed to check her backpack) caught up to her sister, Alexis had donned a sunhat and shades and was impatiently trying her cell phone.

"It doesn't work. I can't believe we don't have service here. How will we call the concierge?"

"Concierge?"

"Of course," Alexis said hurriedly. "The concierge of the hotel will dispatch a taxi for us."

"But, Lexy, we don't have a concierge. We don't have a hotel. We don't even have a phone number to call."

"Oh," Alexis said, stunned. She'd been so certain about the end result of this trip that she'd forgotten the details. She'd forgotten to do everything right! She felt her throat constrict as the airport cleared out; all the other travelers had remembered to book a hotel.

Helene threw down her backpack. It was heavy with books she thought she would read on the yacht. It was just as much her fault as Alexis's that they had nowhere to go, but she felt angry at her sister for looking so rested and put-together.

Alexis, for her part, was annoyed with Helene. What's the use of having a know-it-all for a sister if she doesn't do the research to find you a place to stay in a foreign land? Alexis put up with Helene continually throwing facts at her: when the Great Fire destroyed London, why Picasso broke with the impressionists, where the Sistine Chapel was located. It was time for Helene to come up with some useful information.

"Go ask that guy for the number of a concierge," Alexis said, pointing with the tip of her sunglasses at the burly man who had single-handedly brought all the luggage out to be claimed; the airport was too small for even one luggage carousel.

"No, you ask him," said Helene.

"You."

This went on for a while until the girls finally realized how seventh-grade they sounded, and Alexis shouted, "Rock, paper, scissors!"

"One, two, three!"

Alexis threw down rock, and Helene threw down scissors. "Watch my backpack," Helene called as she went to speak to the Maltese man.

When she'd finished her question, he looked confused, even though Laszlo had assured them that absolutely everyone on the island spoke English. Finally, words poured out of him. "Well, Miss, thanks to the Smarties Grecian Mediterranean Cup being relocated from Greece to Malta, all the hotels are completely booked."

The man's voice boomed. Helene took a step back. "Yeah, everyone wants to see Great Britain's supposed future king, although God knows they'd better get rid of the monarchy before it's his turn. Can you believe it? A country still run by a queen? How totally backward. How infantilizing!" He shook his head in dismay before continuing. "And don't expect to see the race either. Only a select few yachts are allowed out on the water, and these have been filled for months. Months, I tell you! Only the elite will be out there. You know, the fancy-schmancy, out-of-our-league types. The entire event is ludicrous. I have absolutely no idea what all these tourists expect to do. Maybe catch a whiff of William's sweat as it travels with the sea breeze, because they'll never see him. He's at sea and they're landlocked. They're crowded shoulder-to-shoulder on the beaches in the sweltering sun. Oh, well, what do I care? Malta runs on tourist dollars anyway. Thanks to you and your little friend over there, I have a job. And what a fascinating job it is. Just what I thought I'd be doing with my English Ph.D. I've never seen so much thrilling luggage. Anyway, have a great vacation, Missy."

Helene ran back to Alexis, who, although she stood across the terminal, had been able to hear every word. "What are we going to do?" Helene asked.

Alexis put on her sunglasses and gave Helene a reassuring nod. "I'm sure something will turn up," she said, although she wasn't sure at all.

Helene sat down on her backpack to wait. After all, what else could they do?

Another plane landed. Its passengers spilled into the terminal and were soon whisked away by taxis dispatched from hotels that were all filled up. Alexis was most disturbed by the beads of sweat dripping down her face. The terminal was not air-conditioned.

"I'm calling Dad," she said, forgetting about her nonworking cell phone as well as the fact that they'd lied to Aunt Barbara about their weekend plans. "He'll think of something."

"Wait," said Helene standing up, "what's that?"

Two men were running toward them, carrying small, square signs. The men were dressed identically: black suits despite the heat, black caps, dark sunglasses. One placard read, WORTH. The other, MASTERSON.

"Sorry for the delay," said a familiar voice. "Your taxi has arrived."

Is there no end to what lovesick British boys will do for two cute American girls? Not only had Laszlo and Simon flown to Malta, but they'd also met the girls at the airport in costume. This was the result of a huge argument that they'd had on the way home from Russell Square. Laszlo wanted to abandon the girls entirely, but Simon reminded him: the grand gesture. The girls were bound to be swept away by the romance of the island, plus the romance of the gesture. Laszlo agreed, but only on the condition that they could dress like chauffeurs. He wanted to make sure the gesture was truly grand; they'd rented outfits in town that morning.

This was what caused the delay, Laszlo explained, out of breath. "Simon's uniform was just a bit too small. That is, the trousers rather suffocated his manly area. And we had to exchange it."

"What delay?" Alexis said, smiling like a pixie. Just as the boys took off their scratchy chauffeur's hats, the girls leaned up to kiss them on the lips. After all, wouldn't you kiss your rescuer too?

They proceeded to have the most wonderful day. The "taxi" turned out to be a red convertible, and Simon drove them to Valletta, the capital city, to sit in a waterfront café and drink espresso.

This was the summer they'd been missing. Helene basked in the colors. White buildings covered the hillside like shelves cluttered with porcelain. Above and below, the town was framed by shades of blue. The sky was a pale cornflower, and the Mediterranean was deep and sultry. It was midday, shadowless; the sunlight was dazzling.

Alexis devoured the summer styles. After spending July and much of August wearing boots and tights, she exclaimed over every strappy sandal that passed along the avenue in front of the café, every flouncy halter dress, every adorable mini and hot-pants.

Malta looked back at the girls. Not just the Maltese men, who stared brazenly as they walked by—but the Maltese boats too. Each fishing boat docked in the harbor had been painted with brilliant primary colors: a stripe of green, a blue keel, a red prow, yellow trim. And each one had a watchful eye painted on the front. "The eye of Osiris," Laszlo explained. "It wards off evil spirits."

Helene melted a little after hearing all that Laszlo knew. Well, from that and the sweltering heat.

In the afternoon Simon and Alexis went off to find a beach, and Laszlo drove Helene to the Hal Saflieni Hypogeum, or as Laszlo described it, "The oldest freestanding building on earth and the coolest thing ever." He was right. Helene grabbed Laszlo's hand as they descended into the cavelike stone temple that had more mystery and romance than Stonehenge.

The couples met back in the Grand Harbor at a fish-and-chips restaurant. "We give them almost two centuries of British rule," Laszlo complained, "and all they have to show for it is our terrible cuisine."

Soon all four were covered in salt and grease. But before they had time to wash their hands, Simon paid and said, "Come on, you guys, we're almost late. Philip said that the *Straw Princess* would set sail promptly at nine. Hurry up."

The girls hurried all right, but they had no idea where they were going. "Who's Philip?" Helene asked, helping Alexis with her suitcases and running after the boys.

"Who's the straw princess?" asked Alexis, who was having a terrible time trying to run while wearing wedge heels. Simon stopped and turned around. He couldn't believe he'd forgotten to carry Alexis's suitcases! Would he ever learn to be a gentleman worthy of her?

"Here," he said, "give me those. Now, didn't I explain this? I've secured two berths on a boat called the *Straw Princess*. I know, it's a strange name, but the owners, the Spring sisters, are pretty odd themselves, as you'll see. They're my dad's clients. The *Straw Princess* is one of the few pleasure yachts that is allowed to watch the race tomorrow. So we've got to get going! We have the last two available berths."

Simon had high hopes for this evening. He and Alexis would "accidentally" end up in the same berth. And then, after such a grand gesture, anything could happen! So when Simon said "two berths," he looked at her meaningfully. But she was too busy squealing with Helene. "A yacht! A yacht! We're going to watch the yacht races. We're going to see William!"

By the time the boat actually set sail, Helene and Alexis were exhausted. They hardly had the energy to mumble "good night" to the boys before tumbling—rather seasickly—into their berth.

Up on deck Simon watched the stars. He was thinking about that morning, when a radiant Alexis had kissed him so lightly, so casually, as if she'd been kissing him for years.

Next to him, Laszlo was silent for once, even when a shooting star swiped like a scythe across the black sky. He was also thinking about a kiss, though not from this morning. He was remembering when he'd asked Helene to the dance and she'd kissed him and kissed him. And then they had kissed some more. There was none of that awkward fumbling of most first kisses. They'd matched so perfectly. He just couldn't figure out why it hadn't happened again. Was it really just because of William?

"Helene?" Alexis whispered into the dark room. "Are you awake?"

"Hmmphhshushmph," Helene responded.

"Helene, something's been bugging me all summer, and I just have to ask you it now so that I can enjoy Malta completely."

"Okay . . ." Helene was blinking in the dark, trying to focus, though she had a good idea of what was to come.

"What happened?"

"He broke code," Helene said softly.

Alexis sighed. The sisters had promised each other they wouldn't have sex until they were married. The promise was their code, and they vowed never to let anyone break it. So far, no boy had tried. They were very upfront in their relationships. They always told boys that this was their vow to themselves. It seemed Jeremy had tried to pressure Helene to do more than she wanted, and you just don't tell Helene what to do.

"He was a jerk from the beginning. I totally should have known." Helene rolled over to face her sister. Her eyes had adjusted to the darkness, and she could see the outline of Alexis's face. "But what was awful was that he was so mean about it. When he realized that I was serious about staying a virgin, he totally flipped, calling me names, the whole nine. I never want to be spoken to like that again. That's why I freaked out about Nigel. He's totally reminiscent of the Jeremy situation. And Nichola is so young!"

"Oh, Helene, I'm so sorry. I wish you had said something sooner, but I get it." Alexis reached out to Helene, and Helene took her hand and squeezed it.

"I just didn't want to bring down the summer because of a stupid boy, you know?" Helene smiled. Alexis wished she could be as strong as her best friend. The two girls felt more connected than they ever had. It was a nice feeling. And then they fell into a very deep sleep.

20

Like Ships Passing in the Day

WHEN ALEXIS GROGGILY climbed out of bed, she was puzzled to find herself in the cutest room she'd ever seen. A desk folded out from the wall. The closet folded down from the ceiling. And the shower was separated from the toilet by a screen. The single window was a circle at the height of her stomach. This was a room for gnomes.

Alexis sunk to her knees to look out the window, and all she saw was blue. A brilliant blue sky that met the bluest sea ever. Of course! They were on their way to see Prince William! Once she got her bearings, Alexis settled down to work. She sealed off the shower and proceeded to spray on a tan. (Hey, what else are you supposed to do if you spend the summer in dreary London? Besides, who does UV anymore?) While it was drying, she carefully applied waterproof makeup. Then came the truly difficult decision: which bikini to wear?

"Breakfast will be served in five minutes," came a British voice from behind the bed. Helene, who had rolled herself up in the covers like a burrito, bolted upright.

"It's only the intercom," Alexis replied, as if she'd lived on a boat her whole life. "But we have to go." With a sad sigh for all the swimsuits left unworn, Alexis chose the Armani string bikini that matched her eyes.

The breakfast room was also built in miniature. Three tiny tables with wobbly legs were dolled up for an extremely formal breakfast. There were fine china and silver, all bouncing around with the motion of the boat. Alexis and Helene hesitated at the door, until Laszlo and Simon stood up and gesticulated wildly.

Unlike in London, the boys were wearing shorts and T-shirts, and the girls couldn't help but notice how good they looked. Laszlo had this amazingly sculpted upper body—the shoulders and forearms of a statue—that he usually hid in a baggy sweater and a jacket. Simon was leaner, but somehow already tan, and his muscular legs had fine blond hairs.

Just as the girls were pouring coffee from a silver urn, three women walked in. They were very short and wore, as if to compensate, very tall hats. Helene, Laszlo, and Alexis had to stuff their fists in their mouths to keep from cackling.

The first woman, who couldn't have been more than four-foot-ten, wore a hat that had been designed to resemble the yacht they were sailing. The brim was sculpted out of straw into a boat's hull, with STRAW PRINCESS embroidered in red. Sails, made of soft white silk, stood up twelve inches. The second woman, who was shorter than the first, wore a seagull in flight, complete with a beady-eyed face in the front and two protruding wings on either side. The whole thing was made of feathers. The third sister had gone for something a little more abstract. Her hat was a three-dimensional replica of Mondrian's famous squares, those white, red, and blue boxes that mean modern art. Hers was done with pieces of stiff canvas coming out of a white velvet stovepipe hat. This was too much for Helene. She put her head on her lap and shook like jelly.

Following the capped ladies was a dour, skinny man. He was nearly seven feet tall. His balding head was bare.

"April owns the boat—she's the youngest sister," Simon explained in a whisper. "But June's husband, Philip, the tall guy, knows everything about yachts, so he is always here. And May can't stand to be left behind. You know middle siblings." He rolled his eyes.

"These are clients of your father's?" Alexis asked. "What exactly does he do?"

"Well," Simon began, "you see—"

"Wait a minute," Helene interrupted, a little too loudly. "April? May? And June?"

"Yes, dear?" All three women turned their Seuss-like heads in the direction of the four of them. "Do we know you?"

Simon stood to make awkward introductions.

During breakfast—an overwhelmingly British event with a fry-up of eggs, bacon, sausages, black pudding, tomatoes, and mushrooms—Helene looked up to find that Laszlo, while keeping a straight face, had balanced the butter dish on his head. She started laughing at his mockery of the hats, but he put his finger over his lips. Without a word, Helene folded her napkin into a peak and balanced it between her pigtails.

Alexis, when she noticed, laughed so hard that orange juice came out her nose, but still Simon was sleepily devouring his fry-up and he didn't look up. Helene kicked Alexis so that she'd understand. Keeping her expression calm, Alexis casually stuck four forks into her hair so that they formed a peak like a tepee.

"Could you pass the potatoes?" Simon asked innocently. No

one answered, and he finally looked up. "Do you like my hat?" Helene asked. "It's new."

"I love yours, Laszlo," Alexis said. "Could it be Gaultier? I see his handiwork in that dish."

"And yours," Laszlo replied, "is so next year. I know all the runway models are doing forks in the spring."

Simon was clearly not amused. "I think the sisters' hats show excellent craftsmanship," he said huffily. "They were clearly made by an expert milliner."

"Sorry, man," Laszlo said, finally removing the butter dish. "I should have known. Hats are your specialty."

After breakfast the boat sped through the open seas. Alexis was sunbathing in a beach chair on the upper deck, and Simon was . . . well, Simon, seated next to her, held *Crime and Punishment*, but his eyes were elsewhere. Helene had been imprisoned by Philip, who was drily telling her all sorts of information she never wanted to know about yacht racing.

"You see, there are four types of handicaps," he intoned. "Each is based on a rating system designed by the Royal Yacht Racing Club. Now, the first one . . ."

Helene wanted to scream, *What about William? When will I meet William?* But she nodded politely.

When the boat came to a stop, Laszlo disentangled himself from the Spring sisters and set about freeing Helene from the grips of dull Philip. Did he walk over and politely say, "Excuse me, I need to ask Helene a vital question"? Did he rudely call, "Yo, Helene, over here. Now!" No. This was Laszlo after all. When no one was looking, he slipped off his Top-Siders, pulled off his T-shirt, and screamed at the top of his lungs, "Man overboard!"

Helene panicked. This was a real ship in the vast ocean. What if Laszlo drowned! She rushed to the railing, but the Spring sisters had gotten there first and their hats blocked her view.

Philip stood behind her. He could see over any hat, and all of a sudden he began to chuckle. The laugh sounded unused, rusty. He must not have found anything funny for a long time. "It's the lad," Philip said. "He's gone for a swim."

"Come on in, Helene," Laszlo shouted. "The water's great."

"You really should take the opportunity to swim in such pristine conditions," Philip began in his monotone. "We have docked for the morning in the famous Blue Lagoon off the tiny island of Comino, which was named for the abundance of cumin that grows on its otherwise barren rocks. The island was first invaded in . . ."

Helene would never learn about this invasion because before he could say another word, she'd stripped to her bathing suit (a black vintage one-piece with a skirt that somehow looked sexier than the tiniest bikini) and descended the narrow staircase on the side of the boat.

"Don't worry," Laszlo called. "It's not that far. Just jump."

Helene smiled to herself. Laszlo obviously didn't know about her years of swimming lessons. She crouched on the stairs, swung her head to look up at the blue sky, and did a perfect back dive into the water.

When Alexis and Simon joined them, the four raced from the anchored boat to a white sand beach. Much to the boys' shame, Alexis and Helene beat them easily. "Americans," Simon said when he finally made it ashore. "You have all sorts of advantages we lack."

The way back winded even Helene, who was captain of the Scarsdale High swim team, and the four collapsed on deck chairs as soon as they got back on the boat. They fell into such a deep sleep that they didn't notice when the yacht started careening through much rockier waters. They woke only when May stood over them, her yacht bobbing on her head, and called, "The race! The race! The race is coming."

In ten seconds, three of them were standing on the aft deck. But Alexis had slipped down to her berth to reapply her makeup and switch into a white crocheted bikini that was definitely not for swimming.

The *Straw Princess,* which had traveled a great distance since the island of Comino, had anchored among a row of other yachts. The onlookers were silent, even the sunburned Spring sisters who refused to remove their weighty hats but were furiously fanning themselves with huge pink fans. The anticipation was palpable.

As the lead boat approached, Philip brought his telescope to his eye and proclaimed, "Why, I do think that's the yacht Prince William is sailing." Helene had begged a pair of binoculars from May, and she leaned halfway over the ocean to get a look at the boat. But before she could see anyone, Alexis grabbed the glasses from Helene's hand.

"Don't look at what you can't get," Alexis said, pushing her sister out of the way. "It will only make you envious. Don't you know you look like Morticia in that suit?"

Helene stood on her tiptoes to snatch the glasses back, saying, "It's not nice to gawk at your future brother-in-law. That's called incest." She gasped; the boat was coming so fast.

Alexis pulled the binoculars away by their strap so they dangled precariously over the water before she clutched them again. Now she could make out three figures. One at the helm. Another adjusting a winch. The third at the prow. They were coming into view. She stood on her tiptoes and kept the glasses away from Helene.

Helene, in desperation, asked Philip a question, and when he bent down to answer, she snatched his telescope.

It happened as quickly as a lightning strike, but they each saw it. Each saw *him*. A white chest. Arms reaching to the mast. Whipped blond hair. He was concentrating ferociously on his job, but both girls swore that when he passed directly in front of the *Straw Princess,* he turned his head and was momentarily distracted by the sight of them.

"Hi!" Helene screamed. She was actually talking to him in person!

"Over here," shouted Alexis.

The man who might be William raised his right hand in a royal salute. It was enough to make you faint. Well, that plus heatstroke and seasickness.

Alexis fell down first. Helene managed to sit down on the wet deck before she blacked out. Next thing the girls knew, they were in the shade of the foredeck, and May and June were pressing cool washcloths to their foreheads. Simon and Laszlo stood over them, offering iced tea.

"Are you okay?" Simon asked worriedly.

"You had us scared to death," Laszlo added.

"Oh?" Alexis asked, looking at her sister. "I think we're doing just fine."

"Couldn't be better," Helene said, picturing William battling the seas, the perfect royal salute.

21

♛

Love's Labors Lost

"HERE'S HOW IT will work, Simon. You tell Alexis that you want to make sure she doesn't faint again, and I'll stay out late on the deck with Helene, showing her the constellations or something. Although knowing Helene, she'll probably identify more of them than I can."

"Why can't I be the one to stay out late on the deck? I'll show the stars to Alexis," Simon retorted. It was after dinner, and the boys had met up in the minuscule kitchen while fetching another iced tea for the girls. They were devising a plan of musical rooms for the evening.

The commotion over William had been a little regretful. When did you see girls make that kind of fuss over a British guy who wasn't a Beatle? But Alexis and Helene remained sweet—and hot. And they'd seemed delighted by the grand gesture. Laszlo and Simon were sure that if they just spent some quality time with them, the girls would forget all about the prince.

In the end, Laszlo's plan worked beautifully—at first. Alexis had a headache and wanted to go to bed early. A few minutes after she left, Simon followed with a glass of water and two aspirin. He never came back out.

Helene dropped onto the bed in Laszlo and Simon's room. Laszlo couldn't believe his luck. He sat down next to her waiting to make his move.

And he waited. And waited. Because Helene, rolling onto her back and resting her head on her hands, had started a deep conversation with the ceiling.

"So I can't believe I finally saw him," she was saying. "I mean it really solidified my feelings. Even though I had the original crush on William, I'd started thinking that I kept liking him only to beat Alexis at something. Because she always wins. Especially when it comes to guys. You know?"

Laszlo nodded. Should he touch her cheek or just lean in for the kiss?

"But now I realize that the bet is only secondary. What's real is my feelings for him. And I can't help but think he might reciprocate. You know when you've liked someone for a long time, you start thinking you hear their voice in your head? And you feel so close to them?"

Laszlo knew. He heard Helene's voice in his head every day; he saw her quick smile, and he heard her crystal laugh. But now she was right here in his room. And she seemed farther away than ever.

"I have a serious question, Laszlo," Helene said, rolling onto her stomach and propping herself up with her elbows. She looked directly into Laszlo's gray eyes, for so long that he thought for sure she was about to kiss him. But then she said, "What do you think it would be like to be in the public eye like that? I mean, what would it do to you to be under such scrutiny?

I think it would make you pretty responsible. More mature. A little sensitive."

"Well, I think you've answered your own question," said Laszlo. He believed that such public attention probably made you a stuck-up jerk.

"It might also make you more alert to the world around you. Like to aesthetics. Don't you think?" Helene continued. And she didn't stop talking about William and his worldly life until two in the morning, when she promptly curled away from Laszlo and fell asleep, dreaming of her prince no doubt.

Meanwhile, a very similar scene was playing out two berths away. Alexis, grateful for the aspirin, perked right up and started talking. About William, of course. How did he learn to steer a yacht like that? Wasn't he talented? Did Simon think that William wanted to sail all around the world? Alexis really wanted to sail around the world, she explained.

"Wouldn't it get claustrophobic?" Simon asked.

"Not if you're with the right person," Alexis said dreamily. "William is definitely the right person. I didn't know that before. I thought that maybe he was too much of a, uh, player for me." She laughed embarrassedly. "I mean, I like a man to be a little more serious. To have goals, you know? But now that I saw him on the yacht, I realize how dedicated he is."

Simon wanted to scream, *I'm serious; I can steer a yacht. My family has its own yacht. It just happens to be off of the coast of Wales right now with my bastard older brother. I'll take you around the world. I'll take you anywhere.* But instead he just said, "Should I get you some more water? You really were dehydrated."

"You're so sweet," Alexis said, briefly grazing her fingers over his arm. "Now, if you were William, what would you do after such a victory at sea? Would you take some quiet time in a villa in Italy? Or maybe you'd want a celebration. But where? Where do you think he's going next?"

And on and on. Until she fell asleep midsentence. Her last words were: "But what was William wearing?" Frustrated and hurt, Simon counted the tiles in the ceiling. There were ninety-three.

"I just can't believe it," Laszlo said. He was talking to Simon on the aft deck before sunrise. Neither had been able to sleep, and they'd bumped into each other roaming the decks and brooding. "We fly to Malta. We arrange a boat for them. And they respond like this. You know, all summer they acted like they really liked us. It didn't seem like a game. William was their little game. But I'm beginning to think they were just toying with us, trying to get things out of us. Perhaps they've been calculating this whole time. I think they're using us."

Simon sighed and slouched against the railing, defeated. His eyelids were pink from lack of sleep, and his hair stuck up on all sides, much like May's hat. "Maybe we're approaching it wrong, Laszlo. I mean, we said earlier we're not just in this for some snogging. Maybe we are . . . I mean *you* are . . . just mad because Helene wouldn't put out."

"Put out?" Laszlo shouted, causing Simon to look around nervously, but all was quiet and dark around them. "Snogging? Look, Simon, I would have been happy to just hold Helene's hand. I mean I can't deny that I *thought* about doing something else. But that's not what makes me mad. It's this toying. This using. Have you ever noticed that they're totally sweet to us, just as long as we keep doing things for them? Especially things that bring them closer to stupid William?"

Simon held his head. He was determined to reason his way out of this. He was frustrated, true. But he didn't want to accept what had happened last night. He didn't want to believe that Alexis really didn't even see him. "I think we're taking the wrong approach. We said we liked being their friends. Well, friends listen to each other. Something big happened to them last night, and we listened, like best friends."

Now Laszlo slumped onto the wet floor, laying his head on the ground and looking up at the lightening sky. "I have a best friend, Simon. You. You're my best friend. I don't need another. When I look at Helene, I don't think 'friend.' I think 'gorgeous.' I think 'perfect.' I think, 'That's the girl for me.' Can you honestly tell me that when you look at Alexis, you think, 'Gee, she'd make a great friend. Perhaps we can play cricket now and then'?"

Simon couldn't deny Laszlo's logic. When he pictured Alexis the way she looked yesterday in her white bikini and with her long dark hair in a ponytail, cricket was the farthest thing from his mind. "You're right," he whispered. "They've gone too far."

Laszlo was back on his feet, pacing back and forth. "We said we'd make a grand gesture to show them how much we adore them. And they don't even thank us. I'm beginning to wonder, Simon, if they're not rather selfish. Are they, despite their obvious charms, just your typical self-centered American girls?"

The girls woke up at the same time, and both famished—but still beaming about yesterday's amazing occurrence—they met up in the dining room, where Simon and Laszlo were desperately drinking coffee as if it were water on a desert island.

"So," Alexis began, "what hats do you think the Spring sisters will be wearing today? A bas-relief of the island of Malta?"

"Oh, I know: William's face made of felt," Helene exclaimed.

The boys said nothing. Alexis was wearing a new polka-dot sundress, but Simon wouldn't look at it. Helene sat so close to Laszlo their arms touched. Laszlo jerked his arm away.

Helene wondered why both Laszlo and Simon were now so sensitive about hats. She picked up a roll and tried another topic. "I noticed that we're back in the harbor already. Are we picking up supplies?"

Again no answer.

Finally the silence was too much, and Simon said, "We'll be heading back out, but we've arranged for Philip to take you to the airport this morning. Don't you have a flight?"

"Well, it's not until eight this evening," Alexis said. "I thought we were going to have another day on the boat."

"And I thought you were coming back to London with us," Helene said, offering jam around the table. No one wanted it.

"Well, we're not," Simon said sulkily.

They ate the rest of their meal in silence.

Helene felt concerned as she was stuffing her clothes in her backpack and performing her entire beauty regimen by putting on sunscreen and lip gloss. What had they done to piss off the guys? She couldn't think of anything. Did she look weird? Did Laszlo suddenly decide she was too fat? She pulled off her tank top and put on a large Yeah Yeah Yeahs concert T-shirt. Then she sat on the bed and waited as Alexis carefully folded all her clothes and laid them one by one in her suitcases.

"I wouldn't think so much about it," Alexis said. "It's morning. They probably didn't sleep well. You never know what guys get upset about. And it's never anything a little charm and attention can't fix."

But as the girls were saying good-bye to the boys at the harbor, Alexis began to see that they suffered from more than morning sulkiness. She tried to be bright: "We'll see you later this week, okay?"

"This week?" Simon asked, blushing. "I think we're actually going to be busy this week. All this week."

"Friday's the dance," Helene said. "We'll see you then, of course."

"Oh," Laszlo said, not nicely at all, "the dance. Now you want us to take you to the dance so you can get another look at your precious William."

"You invited us," Alexis said. "It's only logical that we thought you wanted us to go. Don't you want us to?"

The moment was tense. Alexis and Helene squinted into the sun to read the boys' expressions. Simon stared at his feet. Laszlo spotted a red flag on a white building up the street. He didn't take his eyes off it as he spoke.

"I think you should consider yourselves uninvited," he said to the red flag. "We'd rather not go . . . with you."

22

The Blame Game

"IT'S ALL YOUR fault." Alexis dropped her suitcases as they reached Air Malta's check-in line. She wiped the sweat from her forehead. Philip had left them in the parking lot, and she'd been suffering, carrying her luggage through the hot sun. "Something happened between you and Laszlo last night, and now the guys are taking it out on both of us."

"Nothing happened. I don't understand it at all. But my only guess is that you were not nice to Simon. They've decided that we're both stuck-up and full of ourselves. But it's not true. It's just you who's stuck-up." Helene groaned as she saw the check-in line. The entire island of Malta seemed to be fleeing at once; the airport was as packed today as the beaches were yesterday, and the line wrapped around on itself like a coiled rope.

"I had a perfectly nice time with Simon," Alexis spat back. "Besides, it's not stuck-up to go after something you want. I wanted to see William, and I did. And if I remember correctly, you agreed that it was the best day of our lives. Better even than meeting Madonna."

Helene had said to Alexis yesterday that the bet over William was the coolest thing they ever did. But maybe that was post-sighting, postfainting delirium. Now it seemed to have messed everything up. She went over all that happened the night before. She and Laszlo had been looking at the stars. They went into his room. She fell asleep. *It must be Alexis,* she decided. *She did something to make us both look bad.* "I had a great time with Laszlo. We just talk—"

Alexis interrupted her. "Yeah, but did you talk about anything besides Prince William and how *thrilled* you were to see him?" Alexis had figured out what she'd done to piss off Simon. And she even felt a little bit bad about it. She liked him too much to make him feel second best. Even though he *was* second best.

But she wasn't going to tell Helene what she'd done. Not unless Helene admitted it first.

"Well, of course I talked about William. I mean we saw him yesterday, remember? Laszlo knows all about the bet. And he's hoping I win," Helene said snottily, kicking her backpack forward as the line moved up two whole feet. "Besides, we talked about tons of other stuff too."

"Like what?" Alexis started to feel worried. She couldn't remember a single thing she talked to Simon about besides William.

"Lots of things. Anyway, I don't have to defend my actions to you." Helene felt hot with embarrassment, but she wasn't going to let Alexis see it. She knew that if she had acted poorly, Alexis had acted worse. That's just how it always was.

"You're always ruining things," Alexis said, so loudly that a Maltese family turned and stared at them. "You giggled too much when we got Madonna's autograph. You told Chelsea

Clinton you wished you had frizzy hair like hers. You never just act normally. I bet when we finally do meet William, you'll say such stupid things that he won't look at either of us."

"Fine, Miss Perfect. How about this? I won't open my mouth anymore." Helene stared in front of her, trying to keep her tears from showing. She'd lost Laszlo and now Alexis. What was happening to her?

They kicked their bags. It was a long line. It was going to be an even longer flight. And unless something changed, it was going to be an extremely long two weeks before they returned to Scarsdale.

23

Chasing the Devil

THE HOUSE ON Whittington Place was dark when they returned. A note taped to their bedroom door read:

> Helene and Alexis—
>
> Saheed and I are at the Orphan Benefit. We're so sorry you couldn't make it, but we suppose Glastonbury is more interesting to people of your age. Basha has the day off. She left a pork roast in the fridge.
>
> Aunt Barbara

"Dinner?" Helene asked, hoping for a truce. The girls still hadn't spoken since Malta.

"Not hungry," Alexis replied, throwing her suitcases on the floor and turning her back to her sister.

The fight apparently had not ended.

Helene slammed the door on the way to the kitchen, stomping

through the peach, mauve, and horse rooms without bothering to turn on any lights. In the kitchen even Mitsy-pooh was quiet. Helene heard the *tick-tock* of the grandfather clock and the hum of the refrigerator. She opened its door and stared at the roast, which looked greenish and a little too porcine to be appetizing. And then, making it even less enticing, the roast began to cry.

Well, something was wailing. Helene heard heaving and sobbing, and it seemed like it was coming from the fridge. Her first thought was, *Burglars!* But why would burglars break in just for a good cry?

But then she heard, "Aw, come on, Nicky. Don't think these fake tears are going to get you out of it. Tonight's the night. That's what you told me."

Helene knew this voice. She closed the refrigerator door and stood as still as possible, listening.

"No, that's not what I told you," Nichola said, still crying. "I don't want to."

"So you've been a tease all this time, Nicky? I've been saving myself for you all summer, you know. I haven't been with another girl. I thought we were going to be each other's firsts. See, stop crying. It's scary for me, too. We'll do it together."

Helene had heard enough. She ran back through the house to her bedroom, ripped the *W* magazine out of her sister's hands, and screamed, "Plan B . . . Nichola . . . Nigel . . . now!"

Standing in the kitchen just outside Nichola's door, Alexis's jaw stiffened with rage. She heard Nigel's voice.

"Nicky, do you want me to tell everyone that you're a tease? 'Cause if you keep acting like this, that's what I'm telling them. You said your parents were out and I should come over."

"But I'm not a tease, Nigel," Nichola said between sobs. "That's the whole point. I'm not ready. You know, I'm only thirteen."

"'I'm not ready,'" Nigel mocked in a falsetto. "'I'm only thirteen.'" He laughed. "Come on, Nicky," he said in his normal, ugly voice. "I see the short skirts you wear. You're asking for it."

"No! Stop!"

Helene and Alexis exchanged looks. Alexis squeezed Helene's hand briefly, and then tried Nichola's door. Thankfully, it wasn't locked.

Nichola was crouched in the far corner of her canopy bed, her arms clutching her knees. She'd pulled her pink quilt over her, and she looked very small. Nigel, also on the bed, was kneeling in front of her.

When he heard the door, he dropped both of his hands to his side and tried to play cool. "Well, look who we have here! Posh Spice. Ready to join the party?"

"Nigel. Please do us the favor of leaving our cousin alone," Alexis said, as if she were talking to a misbehaving grade-schooler. Nichola, whose face was streaked with tears and running mascara, giggled in spite of herself.

"Uh, I was just telling Nichola good-bye. Wasn't I, Nichola? I was just leaving. I'll leave. Just having a good-bye kiss." Nigel stood up and frantically grabbed his jacket from the floor.

"Not so fast, Nigel," Helene said, walking into the room and standing next to her sister. "You're not leaving. Alexis and I have a few things to tell you first."

"I'm late already. Another time."

"Number one," Helene said, leaning against Nichola's wall. Her heart was thumping, but she needed to be calm in order not to mess this up. She tried to imitate Alexis, who could remain collected and detached even if the ceiling were caving in. "Please don't ever come to this house again."

"Number two," Alexis said, smiling sweetly, "never call Nichola on the phone. She's much too good for you."

"Number three," Helene said, mimicking Alexis's soothing tone, "if a girl says no, she means no. And anything you try after that is sick, illegal, and totally messed up."

"Number four," Alexis said, walking around so she stood directly in front of Nigel, "I need to talk to you about fashion. I am, as you may know, an expert."

"What's wrong with my look?" Nigel said impatiently.

"I couldn't care less about *your* fashion," Alexis said, looking distastefully at Nigel's coat, an expensive Armani item he clearly ripped and stained to look cheap. "I'm talking about Nichola. What Nichola wears has nothing to do with you."

"Uh, Alexis, is this—" Helene had to interrupt. But Alexis put a hand up to quiet her.

"It's quite necessary," Alexis said to Helene. Turning back to Nigel, she continued. "Now when artists like Marc Jacobs and Zac Posen design clothes, it's someone like Nichola they have in mind. So when she wears a miniskirt or a strappy tank, she's not saying that she wants to have sex with you. She's not saying anything to you at all. She's just wearing clothes."

Nichola was beaming. She looked like a little girl who'd just received a pony for Christmas.

Nigel crouched on the pink carpet to tie his boots. Helene left the safety of the wall and stood over him. She felt like she had to be a little more explicit. "What she's saying, Nigel, is that a girl in a miniskirt doesn't want to sleep with you. No one wants to sleep with you, Nigel."

Nigel looked up and whined, "But she *said* tonight would be the night."

Alexis shook her head impatiently. "Come on, Nigel. Let me do the honor of escorting you out of the Hussein house."

As Helene jumped on the bed to talk to her cousin, Alexis

distastefully held Nigel's coat between forefinger and thumb and led him through the many rooms to the front door, letting go only when he crossed the threshold.

Alexis watched Nigel walk down the path. She needed to sit Nichola down and have a chat with her. She had meant what she said to Nigel, but Nichola *did* dress quite inappropriately sometimes. She was such a beautiful girl and it was such a shame to see her looking trashy.

When Nigel reached the sidewalk, he paused and turned around. His bashful, hangdog expression was gone, and true to form, he had a little sneer on his face.

"Remember," Alexis warned, "you're not allowed back on the property."

"Well then, Lexy," Nigel called back, "you'll have to come over here. There's a little something I think you'll be interested in."

"Good-bye, Nigel. I'm going inside now."

"It's about William," he said, lowering his voice so she had to strain to hear. "Prince William, that is."

Alexis hated herself more with every step she took down the walkway. *Why am I doing this?* she asked herself. *He's a total sleeze. Why am I listening to him?* But the call of William was too great, and soon she stood next to Nigel on the sidewalk.

"Don't worry, Lexy; I'm not going to bite," he said, cackling.

"Please," she said, trying to maintain her calm, "never call me Lexy again. My name is Alexis."

"I thought, *Alexis,* that you might be interested in this." Nigel reached into the pocket of his ridiculously reinvented coat and pulled out a flyer. "It's a little party I'm throwing. On Friday night."

"That's the night of the end of summer dance," Alexis said, remembering with a hot flash of shame how she'd been uninvited to the dance.

"Exactly," said Nigel, holding the flyer for her to see. "And this is the anti-dance. I'm so sick of the stupid dance with its formality and sappy themes. So I'm throwing an alternative party at my house at the same time. And here's a little secret: Your friend William promised to attend. He's over the dance scene as well. All the same girls, he said to me. So, Posh, don't you want to win the bet? It shouldn't be hard. You're much more beautiful than Helene. You just need to be in the same room with William. And you can be, if you do what I say."

Alexis reached for the flyer, but Nigel lifted it out of her reach. "How can I believe you?" she asked. "How do I know you're not lying to me about William?"

Nigel smiled. He slowly dipped back into that disgusting coat and came out with his cell phone. "Listen to this," he said, dialing voice mail and handing his phone to Alexis.

"Nigel. It's Jont. Got the flyer for your party. It's rad. Forget the dance, I say. Tim's coming too. And Justin. And even Wills said he'll make it, so you know it's gonna be legit. Later."

"That's your Wills," Nigel said, snatching his phone back. "Now, don't you want to see the flyer."

"Sure," Alexis said, staying calm as a doll although inside she was screaming. *They were talking about William!* She reached again for a flyer, and again Nigel raised it above her head.

"Say you want it, *Lexy*. Say you want it. Tell Nigel you want it."

Alexis would never, ever say those words to Nigel, so she came up with another tactic.

"Look!" she screamed, pointing down the street. "The cops. Helene must have called them."

Nigel spun around, and Alexis grabbed the flyer out of his hand. She turned and walked up the steps as he nervously sprinted away.

24

♔

Nichola Gets Smart

"ALEXIS, DARLING, WHY don't you pack up early?" Lady Brawn was saying as she checked the layouts for the September issue. "I can finish this up myself. I don't want to get too dependent on you, now that you're leaving us tomorrow."

"Sure," Alexis said, tying her coat and trying to look pleased. The truth was, the offices of *Vogue* were the only place she felt the slightest bit happy these days. At home she and Helene were still barely on speaking terms. Nichola, newly released from Nigel's clutches, was following Helene around everywhere like they were best friends. And it's not even worth mentioning Simon and Laszlo. They still hadn't called. She and Helene were leaving next Wednesday, and this summer was coming to a truly depressing conclusion.

Well, she thought, waving good-bye to the receptionist and exiting *Vogue*'s forbidding doors, *a mood like this calls for a little shopping therapy.*

Alexis stood on the curb waiting for a cab. She'd shoved one hand in the pocket of her Burberry coat, and she could feel a piece of paper. Now, as a rule, Alexis never, ever kept anything in her pockets. It broke the line of the garment. So she pulled it out immediately. It was Nigel's Xeroxed flyer.

THE ANTI-DANCE
COOLER, BADDER, DRUNKER
THIS FLYER ALLOWS YOU AND ONE FRIEND ONLY.

Helene would have pointed out that "badder" was not actually a word. But Alexis only stared at the black scrawl and thought, *William.* This summer was not over for another week. And the bet didn't end until the plane ride home.

Alexis took a cab to the Mayfair district and walked into the first store she saw, determined to find the perfect item of clothing, the one that would alter her mood and win William's adoration. The store was called Yolk, and as in most fancy stores, only about six things hung on the racks. Usually Alexis drooled over each one.

Not today. The seams were uneven. The blouses cost two hundred pounds and had only one sleeve. This whole eighties fashion thing seemed, for the first time, a rip-off. The pants and stilettos were just like pants and stilettos in every other store this summer.

"Thanks," she called to the shopkeeper.

She tried the next store. The same thing happened. Everything was totally nice. The silk was heavenly soft, and the cuts were just right for the season. But nothing would salvage her mood. Nothing would win William. Nothing would work as her talisman.

For a few minutes Alexis stood outside on the street. It was early dusk, and it had begun to rain. The streets were filling up with after-work shoppers. Elegant women, wearing all the clothes she'd just seen inside the shops, rushed by, swinging bags that held more of the same fashionable clothes. Alexis watched in awe and confusion. She had a deep longing to run home, grab Helene, and call off the bet. Then they could be best friends again. Then they could call Simon and Laszlo and apologize for their behavior. The four of them could order pizza and spend the evening watching reality TV.

Stop it, she told herself harshly, then looked around to see if anyone noticed she was talking to herself. You are Alexis Worth. You love to shop. You will find the perfect item. You will look gorgeous in it. William will take one look at it and fall in love. Helene will be so happy for you that she'll be your best friend again. We'll both move to London to be with William. Then Simon and Laszlo will still hang out with us, because they are cute and fun.

And with that pep talk, Alexis returned to the stores. She was, as Hugo Worth often said, determination personified.

Meanwhile, back at home, Helene was despondency personified. She sat in the mauve living room and picked up a book, only to throw it down, disinterested. She brought her sketch pad and pencils to the peach room, where there was better light. But she managed to draw only a black circle in the middle of each page, sighing all the while.

Aunt Barbara, who had been watering the geraniums, paused in the doorway and watched her niece. Helene had been like this for days. This normally bubbly, sunny girl was now moping like Nichola. (Aunt Barbara was not the most perceptive woman on the planet, so if she noticed Helene's mood, it had to be bad.)

Barbara couldn't take it anymore. Helene was her sister's daughter, her responsibility. Surely there was something she could do. Something like . . . tea!

"Helene, honey," Barbara began, "I can't stand to see you sulking like this. Even the flowers are starting to droop in sympathy. Come and have a nice, warm cup of tea with me in the kitchen."

Aunt Barbara had adopted the British belief that tea could fix most things that ailed you. Helene had no choice but to comply. She tore out each drawing of black circles, crumpled the pages, and followed her aunt into the kitchen.

"Now," Barbara said, pouring Helene a mug of tea and filling it to the brim with milk and sugar. "Tell me why my happiest niece is suddenly Miss Darkness."

Helene sucked in her breath. She didn't want to talk to anyone. She just wanted to storm around and feel bitter and sorry for herself. But Aunt Barbara was looking at her with the same eyes as her mother. She was stroking Helene's forearm, just like Helene's mother did. And suddenly Helene couldn't contain her sorrow anymore.

"Alexis and I have this stupid bet, and it's tearing our friendship apart," she said, feeling like a wave was crashing inside her. "We promised to dedicate this summer to catching this one guy. But there's another guy who I really like, Laszlo. He's just so great. He's cute and funny and weird in a way that I really appreciate. He doesn't just do the normal thing. He turns every one of your assumptions on its head. He's mature that way. Anyway, I really, really like him. And he was going to ask me to tomorrow's dance. But I totally ruined it because of the bet. He thinks I don't like him."

"So why don't you end the bet?" Aunt Barbara asked.

"I can't," Helene said, and she started bawling. "I can't because Alexis won't. And so if I call it off, then she'll go ahead and win. And she always wins everything. I had a crush on William first. And if she takes him, then maybe she'll start taking everything that's mine. Like maybe she'll start dressing like me and painting and getting good grades, and then our friendship will be over. We'll be competitors and not best friends."

Aunt Barbara handed Helene a tissue. This did seem like a bind. She could see how determined Alexis was; it would be hard to lose a bet to a sister like that. "Well, Helene," she said, offering all she could think of, "how about another cup of tea?"

Nichola had her ear pressed to her bedroom door. Some words were muffled. Like did Helene say "painting" or "fainting"? Was that "moneylenders" or "competitors"? But she got the general gist. And there, sitting cross-legged on her pink carpet, she decided to repay her cousin for helping her escape Nigel.

"Alexis, please pass the potatoes," Uncle Saheed said. "And a smile would be good with that too. You've been sulking all week, I dare say."

Alexis pressed her lips together in a weak imitation of happiness. Nichola sighed. They were stuck in the middle of another interminable formal dinner. Helene wouldn't look at Alexis, and Alexis wouldn't look at anyone. Nichola had been patient through the soup, the salad, and the roasted chicken. But if her parents thought she was going to sit quietly while Alexis pressed her bread pudding into her plate without eating a bite, they were sorely misguided.

Nichola covered her mouth and started an exaggerated coughing fit. "Oh, my," Barbara said, "pass her some water."

Nichola sputtered out the water that Helene offered. "Can I be excused?" she asked, coughing all the while.

"By all means," said her father, "but be back for the cheese course, Nichola. I bought a quince jelly especially for you."

Nichola rushed out of the room, hoping no one would notice

that she was headed in the opposite direction of her bedroom.

Luckily, Helene's messenger bag was right on her bed. Unluckily, it was the messiest thing Nichola had ever seen. She sorted through a stew of paintbrushes, newspaper clippings, notebooks, tampons, lip gloss, sparkly bracelets, folded notes, letters from America, two-pound coins, and journals until she found, on the very bottom, Helene's cell phone.

Nichola clutched it as if it were the most valuable thing in the world. Which it was. The dance was the next day, and there was no time to spare. Nichola escaped into her cousins' bathroom, which was almost as messy as Helene's bag. She turned the sink on full blast before she dialed, so no one could hear her talk. You can never be too careful.

He answered right away. "Helene, I was hoping you'd call."

"It's not Helene. I'm Nichola. I'm not sure if you know me. But I know who you are. I know quite a lot about you." She affected Magda's worldly accent and tried to sound as mysterious as possible.

"Oh. Her number showed up. I got confused." He sounded disappointed. "Of course I know you, you're Helene's cousin. But why are you ringing me?"

"I have something important to tell you. But I don't have much time. So please listen."

"I'm trying. But it's so noisy. Where are you calling from?"

Nichola looked at the sink. "A river. I walked all the way to a waterfall to call you. It's *that* crucial that you receive this information. So please listen carefully."

She proceeded to tell Laszlo everything she'd heard Helene tell Aunt Barbara, returning just in time to spread quince jelly on romano cheese. She was the only one at the table smiling.

25

♛

Reinvited

"GIRLS, PLEASE REPORT to the front office in five minutes. Wrap up your final duties, and do not arrive late to your good-bye tea."

Even Ms. Ming's invitations sounded like commands. As she strolled out of the office to prepare the tea, two of the four interns hurriedly cleared off their workstations so that no trace of them would be left in the National Gallery after their summer internships ended that afternoon at five. But Helene, who had left a rather large mess of sketches, doodles, and unrelayed phone messages covering her workstation, had something else to take care of.

"I'll be back soon. Can you tell Ms. Ming I'm in the bathroom?" Helene called as she slipped out the back door and into the walled-in courtyard the staff used for cigarette breaks. Crouching behind a particularly large hedge, Helene took her cell phone from her pocket. She'd gotten a message from Laszlo this morning. It was totally out of the blue. And totally exciting. After they said their "heys," both Laszlo and Helene spoke at once.

"I have something to tell you," Laszlo said to Helene.

"I have something to say to you," Helene said to Laszlo.

There was a long awkward silence, broken by Helene's laughter. "Okay, you go," she said.

"No, you go," said Laszlo. Helene paused. This was the most uncomfortable conversation the two had ever had. "I'm sorry for how I acted on the boat. Getting all worked up about William and totally ignoring you and not—"

"No," Laszlo interrupted, "you and Alexis were just having fun. William was your game. I shouldn't have taken it so seriously."

"That's very generous," Helene said. "But come on, I was acting like a self-centered jerk."

"You're right," Laszlo said soberly. "You were acting exactly like that." Although he agreed, he didn't want to hurt Helene's feelings. To him, she was an angel.

"How come you're not joking around?" Helene asked. "You usually turn everything into some big joke. This isn't like you."

At this Laszlo laughed. But only briefly. "I can't laugh. What I have to say is much too important. I'm scared unfunny."

When he said this, Helene also got very scared. She stared at the cigarette butts stuck between the bricks. She heard her pulse fill the courtyard. Was he going to tell her that she'd acted unforgivably? Was he going to cut her out of his life completely?

"I want to tell you," Laszlo began. "I mean, I want to ask you—"

He paused. Helene helped him out. "Maybe you should speak in your fake foreign accent. That might help."

"A splendid idea. Okay, here goes: I am wishing to be saying to you. You are to be coming along with me to be having the fun."

"The fun?" Helene giggled. This didn't seem bad.

"Yes, to be having all the fun at the cat party."

"The dance?" Helene asked. "You still want to go with me?"

"Of course I want to go with you," Laszlo said, slipping back into his British accent. "I would rather eat cement than go with anyone besides you."

"But it's tonight!" Helene said, so relieved that the words came out in a rush. "And I have absolutely nothing to wear. I don't have a fancy dress or anything. And it's a formal dance. And I have pink hair! I got some funny stares at the Royal Ball and I'm—"

"Baby," Laszlo said, causing Helene's heart to jump, "you look better than anyone even in a T-shirt and jeans. Just come dressed as yourself."

"Are you sure?"

"How about this? I'll make sure that you look just right. It's a surprise. So . . . I'll pick you up at nine?"

"And Simon—is he calling Alexis?"

"At this very moment."

Helene transformed into a bird. A dove perhaps. She flew back into the National Gallery, waving her wings at the sour security guard and landing in the front office. At least that's how it felt. She couldn't tell that she had feet or legs.

The tea was well under way. The other interns were seated on folding chairs, holding their china on their laps, and gracefully sipping cups of sweet, lukewarm water. In the center of the room was a table with a thin apple tart that no one had bothered to serve. Ms. Ming stood with her arms crossed next to an empty chair, presumably Helene's.

Helene shook her wings as she landed. Then she rushed over to Ms. Ming and kissed her on both cheeks. "Thanks so much for a wonderful internship! I'm going to miss all of you." She kissed the interns on their foreheads and laughed at their shocked expressions. "Cake, anyone?" she asked, cutting the crumbly confection into large triangles.

Trafalgar Square was the girls' favorite spot in London. If you stood at the statue of Lord Nelson, you could see the whole city rush by. There went punks and businessmen and high-fashion ladies. Here came black cabs and bike messengers and minis. Surrounded on all sides by ornate gray buildings, the gray sky made sense, and London seemed the center of the world. Alexis had received Helene's text message just as she was leaving work: *Meet me at Nelson. We've got to talk.*

Alexis supposed that their silent fight was over. She was relieved. But she was also glad that she hadn't been the one to initiate communication. She liked to stick to her guns. Or rather, to her Jimmy Choos, which had been a good-bye present from Lady Brawn.

"Oh, Lexy, isn't it amazing?" Helene crooned as soon as Alexis approached. "We have a few days just to enjoy London without working. And the boys are our friends again. Well, more than friends."

"Mmm." Alexis made a noncommittal noise. *This* was why Helene wanted to meet? Alexis was preoccupied; she had to choose an outfit for Nigel's party—or as she considered it, her Last Chance.

"Aren't you excited?" Helene asked, twirling around and watching the throngs stream around her.

"Sure." Alexis shrugged.

Helene stopped spinning. "What's come over you? Aren't you psyched? There's only four hours until the dance. I thought we'd discuss what to wear."

Alexis couldn't believe it. Helene was just going to forfeit the bet? She pulled out the flyer for Nigel's party. "Don't you remember I told you about this?"

Helene nodded. After they'd rescued Nichola, Alexis had resumed friendship with Helene long enough to tell her about Nigel's anti-dance. Helene hadn't even considered going. It was at Nigel's house, for goodness' sake. Anything having to do with him was poisoned. "But, Lexy," Helene protested, "that's Nigel's party."

"Well, I left something out when I told you about it." Alexis paused for dramatic effect. "William's going to be there. I'm sorry I didn't tell you earlier. But Nigel gave me proof."

"William! But, Lexy, he's going to be at the dance. I totally forgot to tell you. Nigel told me way back at Jont's party!"

Alexis gulped hard. "Who's Nigel lying to?"

Helene laughed. "It doesn't matter anymore. Because I realize it was Laszlo I liked all along. I'd rather see him than a million princes."

Alexis ignored her sister. She was pacing back and forth. "Nigel could have been lying to me, I suppose. But Jont's party was before Nigel decided to throw the anti-dance. No, I'm going to have to hope he told me the truth. I'll take the risk."

"What are you talking about? Didn't Simon call you?"

"Of course. But Helene, I had a goal. My goal this summer was to meet William. Well, to *catch* him and . . . you know. And so was yours. And I for one wouldn't be happy if I returned to Scarsdale having done any less. I'm not the type to settle. So should we go home? I have to blow-dry my hair. And you have to do *something* with yours if you're really going to that dance."

Helene walked with Alexis to the Tube, feeling like her wings had been clipped. Her feet dragged heavily and her head spun. The summer felt unresolved. She might never know what would have happened if she'd met William—her William. And she would never find out who William would choose. Maybe Alexis was right.

26

In Which Alexis Meets Her Prince

VAMPY GLAMOUR. Remember that? Well, in the previous few weeks, Alexis had mastered it. When Saheed dropped her off at Nigel's party high on her Jimmy Choos, Alexis's black leather pants fit perfectly, and her wrap top looked shimmery and fresh. Her makeup was simple: bright red lipstick. She'd curled her hair so it cascaded down her back in loose ringlets.

Nigel's house, not surprisingly, was outlandishly posh. If Alexis was rich rich and Aunt Barbara rich rich rich, then Nigel was ridiculous. He'd spray-painted THE ANTI-DANCE on three white sheets and hung them over the two-story living room, which was rapidly becoming trashed. The house was packed and the music pulsing, but still, if you listened hard, you could hear a collective gasp when Alexis entered the dining room. It sounded like all the tires on all the cabs in Trafalgar Square deflating at once. Soon the line to talk to Alexis was longer than the line for the bar. And by eleven-thirty Alexis had been chatted up by a young lawyer, an Oxford freshman, a duke, a few bankers' sons, a boy claiming to be the son of the queen of Tanzania, an heir to the Big Wheel fortune, a Danish exchange student, and at least twenty eager Eton graduates. Everyone had tried to impress. Everyone, that is, except William.

"That's so interesting about your dad's investment company," Alexis said to one suitor, "but I have to run to the bathroom."

Something in the dark hallway had caught her eye. Blond hair. Square shoulders in a perfectly tailored Ralph Lauren shirt. The hint of a smile. Unmistakably William.

Her heart clenched. With shaking hands, Alexis touched his elbow gently. "Excuse me," she said, "do you know where the bathroom is?"

Oh, my god. Alexis was talking to the heir to the throne about bathrooms! Still, even the coolest girls can lose their cool.

William looked Alexis up and down. Then up again. Then down. Finally, his eyes rested on her chest. "I might show you the way."

He had her by the arm. "I don't believe we've been introduced. What's your name? I'm assuming you know mine."

"Alexis. I'm Alexis Worth."

"You can call me Wills."

His hand wandered slowly down her arm to her back, stopping on her leather pants, just above her bottom.

"Hi, Wills," was all she could muster.

"Well, Alexis Worth. How would you like to come away from all this hubbub with me? There's a car waiting outside, and I know the perfect place to take a girl like you."

Alexis had the strangest feeling. This was like talking to a politician. His smile was charming, sure. His suaveness felt stiff and forced—so unlike Simon, whose nervousness was warm and endearing. Wills's eyes were dull, totally unengaged. Even his tousled hair looked sprayed into place. And what did he mean by "a girl like you"? Was there somewhere he took true girl-friends and another place he took the vampy, glamorous girls he met at parties? And did any of it matter? It didn't matter if he were a prince or not. He still wasn't Simon.

"Thanks, Wills," Alexis heard herself say. She didn't plan what came next. It just came out. "But I have somewhere else I have to go."

27

♛

In Which Helene Meets Her Prince

THE SUMMER'S END dance always had a theme. Remember, this wasn't a high school prom. There was no underwater theme. No rodeo dance. No fifties flashback dance. This was the last event of the summer season for teenage members of high society. Last year the theme was periwinkle. The balloons, cloth napkins, and floral arrangements were that putrid, purply color. Yes, the excitement never stops at the dance. Two years ago the theme was silver. Pretty jazzy, huh? And this year, the theme was black and white.

That's right. The circular tables that ringed the dance floor were topped with black runners and bowls of white gardenias.

The seventeenth-century ballroom, where the party was held, was decked out in streamers the color of newsprint. All the country's richest and snobbiest girls were wearing floor-length white or black gowns. And their escorts, heirs to industry or relations to royalty, wore white tuxedos.

This meant that if you somehow climbed to the dizzying top of the chandelier and looked down, the dance would resemble a chessboard. White pawns, black dukes. White squares of tile, black squares of table. You might find it terribly monotonous. Or perhaps you'd consider it the utmost in symmetry and order. But in any case, your breath would catch in your throat when two newcomers took to the dance floor. You'd see this: bright pink hair and bubblegum-colored dress, deep blue hair and baby blue tuxedo.

It was an act of love unmatched in history. Laszlo had dyed his hair for Helene, to make her feel at home.

He'd picked her up early, when Alexis had just begun the arduous process of curling her bone-straight hair. Once Helene had stopped screaming about his hair—which looked amazing, by the way, against his pale skin and blue eyes—she had kissed him. Then he drove her to a thrift store in Camden, where she picked out a pink prom dress from the fifties. It had a tight corset, stiff tulle for a skirt, and it fit perfectly—if you don't mind a few holes here and there. Laszlo found a ruffled tuxedo that must have been worn by a member of a mellow seventies rock quartet. The Crooners. Or the True Blue Lagoons. Or something similarly cheesy.

Fully outfitted, they picked up Simon, who immediately dubbed them "king and queen of the freak prom." He was wearing a white tux, and with his blond hair he looked, Helene had to admit, totally hot. That is, if you ignored the expression of utter dejection on his face. Laszlo had convinced Simon to go to the dance and meet someone new, but Simon planned to hate the entire experience.

"How about her?" Laszlo asked, pointing to a pretty brunette sitting by herself across the room.

"No," said Simon glumly. He'd been sitting at this table the entire evening, looking as if he wanted the floor to open up and drag him under the earth. Helene and Laszlo had been dancing since the moment they walked in, and now, two hours later, they were out of breath and exhausted.

"If you don't ask that blond girl chatting with her friends to dance, I'm going to go ask her for you, and I'm telling her about your history of scabies."

Laszlo got Simon to smile but couldn't convince him to set his sights on any other girl besides Alexis, who was, as Laszlo pointed out and Helene agreed, a lost cause.

"Fine, then I'll pretend I'm a girl, and you ask me to dance. Just for practice. Oh, Simon, please ask me out. I love the way you waltz."

Helene started laughing. "You boys do what you need to do. I'm going outside to get some air. This high-fashion gown is made of the finest polyester."

On one side of the ballroom French doors led to a stone balcony that overlooked the Thames and across to the lights of South London. Helene ran out, unaware that she was still smiling from all that dancing, unaware how much like a fairy sprite she looked in her poufed dress and with her pink and yellow streaked hair.

"The Thames," she called, thinking she was alone, "I love you! I love you!"

But she wasn't alone. A man was leaning against the far railing of the balcony, hidden in the shadow. "I saw you dancing," he said. "I couldn't keep my eyes off you."

Helene looked over and felt like she was falling. Falling over the balcony, flying over the Thames, melting into the flickering lights across the river. It was William. Her William.

"Are you?" she asked, forgetting all decorum, forgetting everything but her months of loving him.

"Who do you think I am?" he asked, and he might have smiled, but it was hard to tell. He stayed in the shadows, while Helene stood in full moonlight.

"Are you?" she asked again. She'd been looking for him for so long. She didn't know if she'd just conjured him up now.

"Of course I am," he said, bowing his blond head in modesty. He was opening and closing a pocketknife. Probably a royal pocketknife.

Helene was so elated, so completely transfixed, that she completely lost her inner censor. She just said whatever came into her head. And that was, "Don't you ever wish you were a river? Like the Thames? Just traveling and traveling and never stopping?"

Her William moved a centimeter nearer to her and looked out at the river. "It's polluted, you know. Diesel waste and sewage. I hated water sports at Eton. You never know what bacteria lurks there. Totally unhygienic."

Helene laughed, thinking this was a joke. She started telling him about herself, where she lived in America, about the disappointing National Gallery internship. She didn't notice that he hadn't asked her any questions. He just stood, opening and closing his knife, looking intently at her.

She did notice the glint of moonlight against the French windows when they opened. And turning to the light, she saw Laszlo standing bluely in the doorway. He looked like he wanted to say something, but she just waved and turned back to her William. This was too important for her to take the time to be nice and civil. This was perhaps the most important moment she had ever lived through.

"Do you want to dance?" she blurted out.

"Oh, little girl. I don't dance."

"But why not?" She couldn't believe this. Not from him. Dancing was maybe her favorite thing in the world. If she couldn't fly, at least she could dance.

"It's boring. It's undignified. Just a means to an end," he said, raising his eyebrows. "And I'd rather just get right to the end. If you catch my drift."

"Wait, wait!" Alexis called as she ran across the ballroom toward the table where Simon and Laszlo were sitting. She held her Jimmy Choos in one hand, and she looked like a gazelle.

"We're not going anywhere," Laszlo called back. Alexis didn't notice his distracted expression. All she saw was Simon, now standing to meet her, wearing a white tux and looking like a prince. No, handsomer than any prince.

He reached out for her waist as she ran up to him. "I'm so sorry," she said.

"There's absolutely nothing to apologize for. You're here now. And I knew you were going to come."

"You did?"

He nodded. "Laszlo was a disbeliever, but not me. I just feel so strongly about you, and I couldn't imagine you didn't feel at least a fraction of that for me."

Alexis answered him with a kiss, and now it was Laszlo's turn to stare at the tile floor and pray that it would open up and let him tumble into the earth.

"It's not midnight yet, princess," Simon said. "There are still a couple more dances. Will you join me?"

"And then I aimed at four ducks sailing across the lake." Helene's William pantomimed the shooting of a rifle. "I had only four bullets. Guess what happened?"

Helene shrugged. He'd been talking about his vacation in Switzerland for about twenty minutes.

"Why, I hit all four birds, of course."

"Did you eat them?"

He laughed like that was the best joke of all. "I left them there. The cook had already chosen to make veal that night. This autumn I'm going stalking again. I usually kill at least twelve stags a season. I collect antlers. Maybe you'd like to join me?"

Helene shook her head. Nothing made her angrier than the senseless killing of animals. She didn't even wear leather! Unless it was thrift.

"Well, then," he yawned, "I guess we'd better get down to business. There's a private room upstairs from the ballroom. I reserve it each year. Why don't you take my key and go ahead? You'll find the stairs by the ladies bathroom. It's totally private."

He dangled a key on a satin ribbon in front of Helene's face. "Don't worry, little girl. Just go upstairs, and make yourself comfortable. There's even a nightgown you can slip into. And a bed, of course. I'll come up in ten minutes. I take these precautions so no one sees us together. You do understand. I have to defend my reputation. I'm allowed my flings, but they must be discreet. And you do have a rather, uh, unusual look."

Helene stared hard at a barge passing on the river. So it had happened. She'd been propositioned by a prince. This wasn't how she'd imagined it. She had never imagined a duck-hunting, deer-killing, self-centered, unadventurous prince. She thought of Laszlo and the way they danced together. The way they fit together. How long had she been gone? He might start to worry.

"Oh, my god," she said, rushing back through the French doors without even saying good-bye to her prince.

She wasn't prepared for what she found back at their table. Alexis, her stepsister, the one who had ditched the dance for Nigel's party, was making out with Simon right in front of everyone. Across from them, Laszlo had taken all of their place cards and was ripping them into a million pieces. He'd torn his own and Simon's and was now working furiously on ripping up the tiny rectangles of hand-made paper that said, in delicate calligraphy, Helene Masterson.

She knew she was responsible for his terrible mood, and she wanted more than anything to rid him of it.

"Hey," she said, touching his shoulder, "I just got stuck talking to the most boring, pompous jerk in the world. And I was wondering . . ." She paused.

He looked up at her with the cutest puppy eyes. "Yes?"

Helene said, "How you do? You being well? Yes? Yes. Good. Excuse, but I help needed."

A flicker of a smile passed over Laszlo's face. "Well, I'd love to offer my assistance, if you'd just tell me how. What kind of help do you need, miss?"

"Help to making the dance," Helene said.

When the music ended, Helene and Laszlo were the last people on the dance floor. Helene tingled with excitement. There was something different about their dancing tonight. It wasn't just flirtatious. It was anticipatory. When he rested his fingers on her hip, it was like a foreshadowing of what would happen later. And when they held hands as they walked to the coat check, it was electric. It was more exciting, more thrilling, than any time she'd made out with Jeremy.

And to think, she told herself, that I almost messed the whole thing up. To think I would like anyone over him, even a prince. But then it struck her: How *had* it happened? Why did Laszlo forgive her abominable behavior on the boat in Malta? Why did he ask her out again?

She asked him these questions, and he blushed. "Well, I found out that you liked me. That you liked me better than you liked the stupid bet with your sister. Even better than William."

"But *how* did you figure it out? Was it something I said?"

A strange expression crossed Laszlo's face, like he'd just tasted some new fruit and he couldn't decide if he liked it or not. "Actually, this was something I wanted to ask you about. Some strange female rang me. She had all this insight about you. I didn't bother to figure out who she was. I just thought she was my fairy godmother or something. Her name was Nichola."

"Nichola?" Helene sputtered. "My thirteen-year-old cousin?"

"Are you sure? She sounded much older. Wiser."

"Well," Helene said, kissing Laszlo's cheek, "I guess she is our fairy godmother."

Simon had wrapped his coat around Alexis and was unsuccessfully trying to hail a cab amid the throng of young socialites trying to hail cabs. Alexis looked at the guys walking around proud as peacocks in their tuxes and thought about the line of boys angling to talk to her at Nigel's party. *My father is the ambassador from Luxembourg. . . . My father is CEO of Protracted Investments. . . . I'm studying to be a lawyer like my dad.* Why on earth did they all think she cared what their fathers did? What a boring, meaningless way for a guy to impress a girl. She had no idea what Simon's father did. Because it didn't matter.

"Hey, Simon," Alexis called.

He came over to her. "We're never going to get a cab. I think I'll be carrying you home, if you don't mind."

"Not at all. I was just thinking. You never told me what your father does for a living. I mean . . . I promise I don't care. I'm just curious."

Simon looked stricken. Alexis's heart quickened. Was his father a felon? A mass murderer? A white-collar criminal? A . . .

"Milliner," Simon said. "He's a milliner. A hatmaker. But not just any hatmaker. No, he's the royal milliner."

He shrugged as if this were the worst profession in the world. "He made all of the Queen Mum's getups. In fact, if you see anything on the head of the royal family, he put it there."

Alexis's eyes grew to the size of the Mediterranean. "You mean he made the hats worn by April, May, and June?"

Simon nodded. This was the moment he'd been dreading. He'd lost Alexis.

"You mean he makes the hats of—"

"Yes! yes!" Simon shouted angrily. "I could probably convince him to introduce you to William. In fact, you'll charm him so much that he'll take you to William's house for tea tomorrow. Are you happy now?"

Alexis shook her head. "I was only wondering if it would be at all possible . . . I know it's an imposition, and really expensive, but—"

"Yes, you can meet William. Yes. Yes. Yes." Simon started walking away. "But leave me alone."

Alexis caught up to him. "No, listen to me. All I want is a hat. A hat like the Spring sisters wore. Something unique."

"Are you serious?"

"I'm so sick of cookie-cutter fashion. And your father's one of the most creative designers I've ever seen. I'd love to return to America in one of his hats. Scarsdale High won't know what hit it!"

While Simon and Laszlo were still trying to hail a cab, Helene pulled Alexis aside.

"You'll never believe who I met."

"Never mind that," Alexis said. "Guess who was at Nigel's party?"

"William!" both girls exclaimed at the same time.

For a moment the two sisters just stared at each other with blank looks on their faces. Then, as if on cue, they both burst into laughter and fell into each other's arms.

"Your carriage has arrived."

Helene and Alexis looked up to see Laszlo waving at them. Holding hands, the two sisters ran to the cab.

"Oh, Lexy, it was so stupid," Helene said as they ran. "He was so boring, and all he wanted to do was—"

"I *know*," Alexis replied. "What did we ever see in him?"

It was a tight squeeze. Alexis on Simon's lap, and Helene with one leg across Laszlo. But no one minded. Helene had both her arms around Laszlo's neck and was making up for a summer of longing. Alexis and Simon were about to accomplish the longest single kiss in history.

The cabbie drove extra slowly. He knew that these kids were in no hurry to get anywhere. He fiddled with the radio dial, hoping to find a station he could stand and, that way, give them a little more privacy. Cricket scores? Too boring. Rap music? It gave him a headache. Ah, there it was: the BBC news. Nothing better. He turned up the volume.

"And in local news, William of Windsor has a bit of strep throat and has cancelled his visit to London for the weekend, . . ." Alexis and Helene turned away from their boys and locked eyes. Alexis's face went slack as the announcer continued, ". . . And postponed all royal duties. William remains in Holyroodhouse, the royal residence near Edinburgh, where he is vacationing with his father, brother, and grandmother. The time is one-twenty in the morning. The temperature is . . ."

"Who cares?" Helene mouthed.

"Not me," Alexis mouthed back. They each knew what the other was thinking: This was the Plan B they hadn't planned for.

And it was better than anything they could have come up with on their own. Plus they were best friends again. And as always, they were sisters.

"I can't believe you're only here for less than a week," said Simon.

"Well, I expect to see you every day until then," Alexis purred.

"And then?" Laszlo asked.

"And then we'll meet up again," Helene grinned. "Next summer. In France?"